IN THE MARKET FOR LOVE

MEGAN SQUIRES

For Jacob and Abby.

SOPHIE

*T*HE CELLOPHANE WRAPPER crinkled in the man's grip as his hands trembled with nerves.

"She's going to love them," Sophie Potters said, nudging her elbow over the armrest that separated their airplane seats. She could see an envelope slipped between the sprigs of greenery and peach dahlias, the name *Lauren* penned in perfect cursive across the paper. "They're beautiful."

"They are pretty, aren't they?" The man's voice cracked and he blew out a breath. Rolling his shoulders, he admitted, "I don't know if I'm more nervous about giving these to her and the question I plan to ask along with them, or about this plane landing! I don't have a lot of confidence in our pilot after all of those unexpected bumps."

"It has been a bit of a choppy flight, hasn't it?" Luckily, Sophie wasn't phased by the turbulence. "If you're asking the question I think you're going to ask, then you've picked just the right bouquet. Victorians often used dahlias to symbolize commitment and dedication. The perfect proposal flower, if you ask me."

The young man's eyes widened. "You know a little about flowers, huh?"

"A bit."

Sophie grinned and as the plane began its gradual descent, she filled the time with stories of her flower farm and the business she'd started just five years earlier. Sophie knew not everyone had the ability to purchase locally grown flowers straight from the source. Even less had the opportunity to grow them—to have their very own flower field of dreams. Looking down at her hands, at her tattered cuticles that boasted dirt-lined nail beds and her fingers roughened from garden work, she realized she possessed something truly special. She couldn't wait to dig her hands back into the rich soil on the precious two acres of her leased Fairvale land.

"Whoa there, big fella!" The pilot's voice crackled through the speakers as the wheels touched down on the landing strip. A raucous and relieved cheer erupted from the passengers. "Welcome to Sacramento, where today's weather is an enjoyable seventy-six degrees with five mile-an-hour winds out of the southeast."

Standing to collect her bag from the overhead compartment, Sophie slung it over her shoulder and smiled down at the man still in his seat. Even though the plane was now on solid ground, worry shrouded his face.

"Good luck with everything. Take a deep breath and just go for it," she offered, hoping to quell his obvious nerves. "And if you happen to need a florist for the big day, you know who to call."

"I appreciate the encouragement. And thank you for

distracting me during that landing. One hurdle down, one more to go!"

Sophie smiled the whole way through the airport, even though she was like a fish swimming upstream. Sacramento, while California's state capitol, never felt like a big, bustling city to Sophie. After all, it was considered by many the farm-to-fork capital of America, and that held an inherent small-town feel in the title alone. But the sheer volume of people in the airport that morning went strictly against that notion. It felt crowded and stifling, like the throngs of bodies squished into a rush hour metropolitan subway.

Grateful she'd only brought a carry-on and didn't need to await the arrival of any checked luggage, Sophie pressed through the melee of people and burst through the automatic airport doors. The balmy, late spring air met her skin like her very own welcome-home embrace.

Of course she had enjoyed her time in Seattle visiting her youngest brother, his wife, and their new baby. But the skies had been consistently gloomy, a dense layer of gray clinging just above the cityscape like a woolen blanket draped over her entire stay.

The Sacramento Valley, on the other hand, was predictable in its mild springtime weather, and something about that certainty was a comfort to Sophie. It made planning her planting schedule a breeze. She'd tilled and amended her soil months earlier and the seeds she placed into the ground shortly after were likely making their debuts as little sprouts at that very moment. She couldn't wait to drive out to the flower farm to take inventory.

Earlier, before takeoff, Sophie had arranged a ride through an app on her phone. It thrilled her to see the sleek, black sedan already waiting along the curb when she exited the airport, as she was eager to get back home and settle into her routine. The driver must've spotted her from afar because he popped open the trunk while remaining inside the cab. She took that as her cue that she wouldn't be receiving any help with her luggage. That was just fine; she'd be able to manage on her own. Sophie yanked her travel bag from her shoulder to stow it away next to a pair of tangled jumper cables and a tire jack. When she slammed the trunk door back into place, she startled, noticing a man lowering into the passenger seat of the same vehicle.

She marched around the car with clipped strides.

"Excuse me. I believe this is my ride," Sophie asserted as she rapped on the rolled up window with her knuckle. She was met with the back of the driver's head, his dark hair swirling into a cowlick like the coil of a cinnamon roll. "Excuse me!" she hollered once more, but the man was engaged in conversation with his passenger and without even acknowledging her presence on the outside of the vehicle, the car lurched forward and pulled away from the curb.

"Wait! Stop!" Calling out, Sophie chased after the runaway car, but it quickly disappeared into the fold of vehicles in airport traffic. She threw her hands into the air like she was tossing confetti, though her gesture was anything but celebratory. "Are you kidding me?"

"Sophie Potters?" A vehicle of a similar make and model two cars back honked its horn, quick beats in a row like an alert from a trumpet blast. The driver leaned out the window and flapped his hand in her direction in an effort to summon her attention. "Are you Miss

Potters?" he hollered, louder this time. "I think I'm your driver."

"Oh, this is just peachy," Sophie muttered, realizing her blunder and the fact that her belongings were en route to an alternate destination and certainly not to her home. "Yes," she said, shoulders slumped with the admission of defeat. "That would be me."

The man stepped out of the vehicle to collect her luggage, but halted when he noticed her empty hands. "Wow. You're a light traveler."

"I'm a tired traveler, which in this case, has suddenly made me a light traveler." Sophie slid into the passenger seat and clicked the belt across her lap. She blew out an exasperated breath that lifted her side-swept bangs from her forehead. "My bag just hitched a ride in another vehicle."

"Huh, that's weird," was all the young man offered as he got back into the car. When he reached over to turn the dial on the radio to increase the volume, Sophie took it as her cue to keep quiet. He wasn't up for forced pleasantries and she was absolutely okay with that. Not that she wasn't a people person, but she appreciated silence just as much as she did a riveting conversation.

That's what she loved about her sweet little patch of farmland. It was an oasis of solitude. She could be alone with her thoughts there and if she wanted to, she would talk to her plants, though she realized there was a bit of crazy associated with that sort of thing. Either way, it was the best—and cheapest—therapy available. Something about connecting with nature was immensely grounding to Sophie. She knew it was a gift to watch these little seeds push up through the earth, breaking the surface with an inspiring determination to turn into something beautiful. That her plants took on a whole new life once they were cut and left her field was just the icing on the cake. She never really knew if their purpose was to bring her joy in the growing or to bring her customers joy in the receiving. It felt like a fifty-fifty sort of thing, and that, to Sophie, was just perfect.

The white-noise music inside the cab and the soft, rhythmically lulling motion of the vehicle must have ushered her into sleep, because before she knew it, the thirty-minute drive to Sophie's small townhome came to an abrupt end. Her driver shut off the engine after he pulled up alongside the curb, the click of unlocking doors startling Sophie awake.

"Alright. We're here." He broke the silence by clearing his throat. "Have a nice day, ma'am." The driver picked up his phone and scrolled, likely looking for the whereabouts of his next client, readying to move on to another job.

"Oh. Yes. Thank you. You have a nice day, too," Sophie replied groggily, her voice thick and unused. It always took her a moment to fully awaken, even after a short catnap. Clicking open the car door and stepping out onto the sidewalk, she caught herself before walking to the back of the vehicle to collect her luggage, remembering she wouldn't find it stowed in that particular car. For all she knew, it was on its way to Timbuktu by now.

She'd be lying if she said she wasn't disappointed that her belongings were likely gone forever. There were only a few outfits—all which could be easily replaced—but her planting journal with five years' worth of notes was in that bag, and although she knew every year was different and required its own provision, that journal was one of her most cherished possessions. It was like a time machine, transporting her back to each growing season through pictures and words documenting her garden's growth in meticulous detail. Heartbroken wasn't the right word, but she was certainly disappointed she'd never hold the leather notebook in her hands again.

"Sophie! You're back!"

Sophie glanced up to see her roommate, Caroline, bounding down the walkway and rushing toward her at full speed. Sophie planted her feet solidly on the pavement, bracing for the impact. Even though Caroline was as petite as could be, her hugs were larger than life. They weren't just gestures of endearment; they were full-on football tackles.

"I've missed you so much!" Caroline squealed as she yanked Sophie into her arms, their cheeks smashing together. She rocked Sophie back and forth with pendulum-like momentum, dancing her across the pavement.

"I've missed you, too, Care. It's so good to be home."

Grabbing her by the hand, Caroline tugged Sophie up the walkway to the porch. She paused as she took hold of the handle to the front door with her free hand. "Take a deep breath, Soph, and tell me what you smell."

Sophie did as instructed, her chest expanding with a massive inhale. The savory aroma of bacon and hash browns infiltrated her senses, a delicious greeting that caused her stomach to growl with anticipation, like Pavlov's dog and his dinner bell.

"Smells like my favorite breakfast!"

"And fresh fruit, too! I visited the Nicholson's yesterday and their stone fruit looks amazing this season. All that rain from last winter has done wonders for their peaches. The sweetest you'll ever taste. The market is going to be off the charts this year, Soph, I can feel it in my bones."

That was music to Sophie's ears. She'd taken over the Fairvale Farmers' Market last year and while it was initially more work than she'd bargained for while still running a flower farm of her own, there was something so satisfying about bringing farmers together to feed their community. It felt like a back-to-the-basics sort of thing, and how much did people need—even crave—that these days? This year's market was set to open the following Tuesday, and while it would be a couple of weeks before her flowers would be ready for sale, Sophie eagerly awaited the grand kickoff.

"You didn't need to go to all this trouble to make me breakfast, Caroline. They fed me on the plane."

"Well, it's technically brunch. And I know I didn't, but I was hungry and I figured you might be, too. A bag of peanuts does not a meal make."

"I suppose you're right. And it's true; I'm never one to turn down food," Sophie said as she elbowed Caroline and followed her into their home. "Especially food that smells this good!"

Caroline's mouth curved up on the side. "I have a confession," she said as she strode into the kitchen to collect two plates from the counter dish rack. She held one in each hand, pausing. "It's not all completely selfless. I'll be a married woman in just over a month and I figure it's about time for a little practice in the cooking department."

"My brother's not a picky man, Caroline. You know that. You've tasted our mother's cooking before. The bar isn't all that high."

While Sophie loved the occasional home cooked meal at her parents', it wasn't the quality of the food that she enjoyed, but the company that always had her coming back for seconds. Her mother would burn a pot of water if it was possible. Culinary expertise wasn't her gift, but what she lacked in talent in the kitchen, she more than made up for in other ways.

She was the type of mother who wore handmade knit sweaters to coordinate with each holiday and saved coupons for the things she knew her children loved, like their favorite laundry detergent or brand of roasted coffee beans. Motherhood was her specialty and Sophie had a sneaking suspicion that grand-motherhood would be an even better fit. Especially since baby Aimee wasn't eating solids yet and couldn't judge her grandma by her less than stellar meals.

Caroline, on the other hand, didn't need to clock any more hours in the kitchen. She was already a skilled baker, the town's unofficial go-to cake designer for children's birthdays and baby showers. She even took on the daunting task of baking and decorating her own wedding cake, something her bridesmaids had unsuccessfully attempted to talk her out of.

Sophie, however, was one of the few who continually encouraged Caroline to wholeheartedly go for it. After all, she would be a hypocrite to do otherwise. She knew without a doubt that should she one day marry, she would be her own florist, assembling all of the bouquets for her bridal party, no matter how unwise that decision may appear. Why on earth wouldn't she contribute her greatest love and talent to a celebration entirely about love?

Taking a seat on the green and blue plaid cushion in

the breakfast nook window, Sophie drew in another deep breath as Caroline settled a plate in front of her. The bacon was cooked to perfection: fatty ribbons curling like corkscrews and golden-crisp hash browns that made her mouth water. Sophie picked up her fork and had to keep her eyes from shutting contently the moment the food touched her lips.

"This really is so good, Caroline. I'm super happy that my brother gets to eat like this every day, but I can't help but be disappointed that it'll be back to granola bars and O.J. for me."

"You know you're welcome to come over whenever you like, Soph. You're family. It's what families do: make sure we all stay fat and happy."

Sophie knew that, and she didn't question Caroline's sincerity at all in offering. But after spending a week with her youngest brother, Scott, and his family, she knew that welcomes inevitably wore out. She hadn't quite worn hers out, mostly because she inserted herself into any situation where they needed help. With a two-week-old infant, there were countless opportunities for that. She took the 2 a.m. feeding shift multiple nights, knowing she'd be able to catch up on her sleep once back at home. Sophie made sure she was more of a help than a hindrance, and she knew Scott was grateful for it.

But there was never a less desirable position than the third wheel to a pair of newlyweds. Though Caroline had started out as Derek's girlfriend, she quickly became Sophie's best friend. The two women were now nearly inseparable. Sophie knew things would change once the wedding vows were exchanged, and she was prepared for —even used to—that. At twenty-seven-years old, she was the only remaining single gal in her group of girlfriends. At a time when wedding invitations showed up in her mailbox on a weekly basis, Sophie was interning with local flower growers, learning how to farm organically and sustainably. She was more concerned about pest control methods than selecting China patterns. Sure, she'd dated— sometimes even had short relationships—but nothing ever blossomed into anything substantial. She was okay with that. Her time would one day come. She just wasn't in that season of life yet.

Throughout breakfast, Sophie filled Caroline in on her Seattle trip. The two huddled together and swiped through the myriad of baby images on her phone, *ooh*-ing and *ahh*-ing at each adorable picture that graced the screen.

While Derek and Scott had been close growing up, the two brothers had a monumental falling out after high school when they started an internet business venture together. The result was not only an empty bank account, but a relationship that appeared to be strained beyond repair. Derek was now an anchorman for the local news station and Scott had retreated up to the Pacific Northwest to pursue his career in copy editing with a prominent Seattle lifestyle magazine. Sophie was often the glue that kept the brothers stuck together, though she had a feeling a new baby in the family could do an even better job of bringing everyone together. Babies just had a way of doing that. After all, a baby was the epitome of a fresh start.

"You think you two will make a trip up there after the honeymoon?" Sophie suggested as she took the empty breakfast plates to the sink to rinse off. "I know Scott would love to meet you and introduce you to his wife and new daughter."

Sophie never wanted to push her brothers into a deeper relationship. She couldn't force something that just wasn't there. But she knew Caroline's heart and her desire for reconciliation between the two men, and she hoped Caroline could be just a little bit of that familial glue, too.

"I've talked to Derek about it, but he's not budging." She looked at the floor when she said in a hushed, guarded tone, "They still haven't even RSVP'd for the wedding, Soph."

"Probably just trying to work things out for a sitter for Aimee. I know Derek and Scott have had their disagreements over the years, but this is a big day. A huge one. I'm certain Scott wouldn't miss it."

"I hope you're right," was all she replied as her gaze switched from the floor to the front bay window which took in all of Hickory Road. Squinting, she craned her neck forward. "Hey, Soph. You aren't expecting company, are you?"

Sophie pushed back the kitchen café curtain, although she didn't have a good view of the walkway, the myrtle hedge lining the path serving as a leafy blockade. "No. Why?"

"Because there is an incredibly handsome man carrying a duffle bag walking up to the house right this very second, and since I already have a handsome man of my own, I figure this one must be for you."

2

COLE

*T*HE TIRE BLOWOUT on Highway 50 wasn't in Cole Blankenship's plans, but it seemed to be par for the course lately. After two delayed flights—one which was later altogether cancelled—a single day of travel had turned into three. The hotel the airline put him up in was fine, but its immediate proximity to the airport made for constant noise that not even the most industrial of earplugs could touch. He was groggy—bordering on cranky—and when the car swerved erratically as the tire shredded into oblivion, Cole was admittedly too tired to even see his life flash before his eyes. It just sort of jogged by, a string of somewhat uneventful occurrences that made up the sum of his existence.

But this trip out to California—this would be the game changer. He had an innate sense about it. For the last five years, Cole had worked under his father, Martin Blankenship, as the junior landscape architect at their family-run Nashville design firm. While his dad often praised Cole's work and ingenuity, he had yet to give him the lead on any major or notable projects. This opportunity to not only design, but oversee the entire execution of the *Backyard and Beyond Summer Showcase* project was his big break. It had to be. Cole could only live in his father's shadow for so long before he either became eclipsed by it, or burst out and shone all on his own.

Once the car had slowed to a stop on the shoulder of the freeway, Cole made sure to shoot up a quick prayer of gratitude for his spared life, and then set right to work changing the tire, since his driver admitted to having no prior experience doing so. Cole's khakis and button down collared shirt weren't the best attire for this sort of labor, but they'd have to do. He rolled up his sleeves to get to work. When he popped open the trunk to locate the tire jack and spare, he was surprised to see a flower-printed duffle bag wedged next to the tools.

"Yours?" he'd asked the driver, raising it up.

"Nope," was the guy's reply. "Someone must've left it in there."

Having had his share of lost luggage, Cole was familiar with just how frustrating it could be. Years back, on a return trip from Australia, the collection of authentic boomerangs he'd purchased for his young neighbor went missing. He'd held out hope that they'd do what they were created to and fling themselves back his direction, but they never did find their way.

By the looks of this particular bag, it appeared to belong to a woman. Even though Cole was currently single, he'd once dated a woman that spent over two-hundred dollars on her cosmetics alone. It blew his mind.

Though the bag was small, there was no telling the value of the items inside.

Once the car was fitted with the spare, Cole returned to his passenger seat position, duffle bag squeezed between his knees and the dashboard. Unzipping the bag, he tried to search through it as noninvasively as possible, but there was an inherent snooping that went along with rummaging through someone else's stuff that couldn't be avoided. Reaching into the luggage, he pulled out a leather notebook and rested it on top. It was thick, extra papers folded and shoved in between the bound pages, and a leather strip wound around the entirety of the journal. Tugging on a strand, he undid the strap and opened to the first page.

This Journal Belongs To:
Sophie Potters
395 Hickory Road
Fairvale, CA 95663

"Hey," he said, turning to the driver. "Do you mind if we take a little detour?"

～

THE HOUSE WASN'T far from his original destination, which was a relief. While he'd wanted to get settled in, Cole knew he wouldn't sleep well if he did nothing to reunite the mystery bag with its rightful owner. This would be his good deed for the day, then he could crash and catch up on the much needed sleep that had alluded him the previous nights.

Lifting his hand to knock on the cheerful mint green door, Cole startled when it swung wide open. His fist hung in the air.

"Hi there," a small woman with a contagious grin greeted. "Can I help you?"

Cole dropped his hand. "Um, yes. Sorry. I'm looking for a Miss Sophie Potters."

The woman backed up and hollered into the depths of the house, "Soph! It's for you. Told you!"

She left the door open while she retrieved her friend, and Cole breathed in the smell of a homemade breakfast, realizing it had been too long since his last decent meal. His mind wandered, thoughts of food making him delirious with hunger, when a woman he presumed to be Sophie stepped into the door frame. She twisted a red and white checkered dishtowel between her hands, then threw it over her shoulder, drawing Cole's gaze up to her face. She was arrestingly beautiful, and even though her wide green eyes looked puzzled, there was a soft sincerity that made her seem instantly approachable.

"Hey there. How can I help you?" she asked, no hint of the wariness or distrust one normally had in their tone when speaking to a complete stranger. She brushed at her auburn bangs with the back of her hand to push them from curtaining her eyes. She was taller than her friend, her skin a rich golden mixture of both sun and heredity, and dark freckles peppered across her nose.

Cole's words lodged in his throat, his foggy head unable to recall the purpose for his visit, her unexpected beauty throwing him for a loop.

"Oh! My bag! Thank you so much!" she blurted, her

eyes locking on the luggage hanging from his shoulder. "How did you find it?"

"Right." Cole yanked off the duffel bag and thrust it out in offering. "It was in the trunk of the car I rode in from the airport. I discovered it when I changed the tire."

"That explains it then."

"Explains what?"

"Why you have grease marks all over an otherwise perfectly pleated outfit," she said, a lift in her voice that suggested a laugh she fought to suppress.

Cole looked down at his pants, suddenly self-conscious about his disheveled appearance. "I apologize; I'm usually more put together than this."

"I'm not," Sophie said. That held-in laugh finally burst forth, sounding the way a blast of crisp ocean air felt: alive and invigorating. "You caught me on a good day. Most of the time, I've got dirt up to my elbows and compost strewn about my hair."

"Oh yeah? What exactly is your line of work?"

"Flower farmer. Just a few miles up the road, actually. You?"

"Landscape architect."

Sophie nodded. "And do you have a name, Mr. Landscape Architect?"

Immediately, Cole's face heated, embarrassed that he hadn't properly introduced himself to the woman whose doorstep he showed up on completely uninvited. He shoved his hand into the gap between them. "Cole Blankenship."

Without hesitation, Sophie took his proffered hand and shook it with firm confidence. "Nice to meet you, Cole.

Sophie Potters, although it sounds like you already knew that."

"I'm sorry. I honestly didn't mean to invade your privacy. I was just hoping to find something with your name on it so I could get this back into your hands."

"I'm actually so glad you did," she said. "That journal in there means so much to me and when I realized I might be forever without it, well, I can't even tell you how that made me feel."

"Hopefully it was only a short amount of time that you had to feel that way, then," Cole said. He smiled and their eyes locked. His stomach flipped, but this time not from hunger. It felt like he should pull from their gaze, but Sophie didn't seem rushed to, her kind eyes holding his for longer than necessary. "Well, I should get going." Cole spun on his heel, breaking their stare, only then realizing his predicament when he looked back at the empty street. "Right." He rubbed the back of his neck with his hand. "I told the driver he could go, so I don't actually have a ride."

"Where are you headed?"

"To a jobsite for a new project of mine. I honestly haven't even checked it out yet. If it's not obvious, I'm not from here."

"I gathered as much," Sophie said, her full lips hooked up on just one side. "I'm happy to give you a ride, Cole. Think of it as my '*thank you*' for making sure my bag found its way back to me."

"I couldn't ask you to do that." While the thought of spending more time with Sophie was an appealing one, Cole didn't want to impose more than he already had.

"It's no bother at all. And you didn't ask, I offered. I was just about to head out, anyway."

He felt like he was overstepping, but Cole would be lying if he said he wasn't grateful for Sophie's unexpected generosity. "You sure it's not an inconvenience?"

"Was it an inconvenience for you to bring my bag to me?"

"No, of course not. It just felt like the right thing to do."

"And this does, too. So let me do it." Sophie smiled again. "Meet me by the garage in just a second. I'll be right out."

Cole lingered on the stoop a few moments after the front door closed shut. The property was a postage stamp in size, but the curb appeal was off the charts. Window planters boasted clusters of vibrant blooms, bursts of color splashed against the gray siding like splatters from a painter's brush. The yard was uniform in layout, a lush green patch of grass on either side of the hedge-lined walkway. Cole followed the offshoot of concrete that led to the single car driveway, and he suddenly realized he had his work cut out for him with his upcoming project. If California homes were this quaint and cozy, he'd have to rework his plan for the *Backyard and Beyond Summer Showcase*. What he'd originally had in mind was opulent and eccentric. He was embarrassed to admit that his perception of California had been shaped mostly by Hollywood with its high society appeal and glamour. Sophie's home, however, felt akin to middle America: inviting and approachable, much like its owner.

The motor to the roll-up garage door caught Cole's attention first, but the low, gravelly rumble of the truck starting up inside caught him off-guard.

"Hop on in!" Sophie shouted as Cole stepped into the

garage. "The handle sticks a bit, so just give it a good yank."

This day was full of surprises, Sophie's vintage truck the most recent surprise of all. Cole's breath caught in his chest and he needed to audibly clear his throat in order to gather his composure.

"Is this yours?" he asked as he opened the door, pulling hard as instructed. He stepped up into the cab.

"What? You think a girl can't drive a truck?" It wasn't an accusation, but more of a jab at Cole's assumption.

"No, I definitely think you can drive it. It's just that I own one nearly identical to this. Haven't seen many of these on the road lately."

"No joke?" Angling her gaze over her shoulder as she backed down the narrow driveway, Sophie's eyes connected with Cole's when she swung back. "You have a '53 GMC pickup?"

"'54 actually, but yeah, I do. Hasn't run for almost five years now, though. Just sits in the garage gathering dust and an impressive collection of spider webs."

"Oh, mine collects the same, even though I drive it every day. Once popped the hood to find an entire squirrel family taking up residence in the engine."

"I bet that was a startle!"

"More for the squirrels than for me. I screamed so loud and dropped the hood on one of their tails. I felt awful for that poor innocent little rodent."

"I don't think it's so innocent to mess with the engine of this sort of vehicle. It's a classic."

"Indeed, it is."

The two sat in companionable silence for several moments. There was a distinct familiarity in riding shotgun in Sophie's truck. Over the years, the hours spent in the office drafting up landscape designs swallowed up any amount of time available to restore Cole's truck. He hadn't thought much of it until that moment in Sophie's cab, realizing the amount of potential his own vehicle had. Were he younger, it would've been a project he would have loved to work on with his dad. That was the sort of thing he'd seen in many movies growing up. Fathers and sons restoring their relationship while they restored old, broken down vehicles. It wasn't as though his relationship with his dad was a broken one, but it was certainly in need of a tune-up.

Sophie slowed the vehicle in anticipation of the upcoming four-way stop. She turned to Cole. "You have an address?"

Cole reached into his pocket to grab his phone. He unlocked the screen and pulled up his email, reading out loud, "439 Harbor Oaks Way."

Sophie's features froze. "Harbor Oaks Way?"

"Yep. You know it?"

Cole could see her forced swallow. "Yeah, I do, actually." She flicked on her blinker. "It's about a ten-minute drive from here."

"That's good to know," Cole said. He noted the grocery store and gas station as they drove, taking a mental snapshot of their locations in town. Once he got a rental car of his own, he figured it would be important to know where to shop and where to fill up.

"What exactly is it you'll be doing there, if you don't mind me asking?" Sophie questioned.

"I don't mind you asking at all," Cole answered. "I'm working with the homeowner to completely redesign their backyard landscaping. New outdoor patio. Huge water feature. All new trees, plants, and shrubs. We'll be entering the *Backyard and Beyond Summer Showcase* at the end of next month. You heard of it?"

Sophie just nodded, seemingly unable to marshal any expression other than the blank one that still coated her features. "Yeah, I've heard of it." Her gaze stayed fixed out the windshield. "And just how *beyond* the backyard will it go?"

Cole shrugged. "I've only seen pictures, but from what the owner has shared with me, it's pretty much my own blank canvas. They've given me free reign over the entire property. It's a landscape architect's dream job, to be honest. I'm a bit like a kid in a candy store with this particular project."

"Free reign," Sophie repeated, as though she needed to say the words again to understand them fully.

"Right? Pretty exciting."

"Pretty something," she said, this time even quieter.

They didn't converse much more after that, and Cole figured Sophie was just allowing him the quiet to take in the new-to-him town and surroundings. When they pulled up to the property, he expected their goodbye to be cordial —at least as friendly as their welcome had been. But when Sophie just offered a tight-lipped smile, Cole worried he had inadvertently offended her.

"Thanks again for the ride," he said, wishing he had luggage of his own to fiddle with, but he'd sent his belongings out the week prior in order to ensure smoother travels. Although that hadn't really turned out to be the case.

Sophie's smile lifted unnaturally higher onto her

cheeks, but didn't reach her eyes the way a sincere grin would have.

"Okay, then," Cole tried again as he stepped out of the vehicle. "Hope to see you around town sometime."

Still smiling her plastic grin, Sophie just nodded and then pulled the truck away.

3

SOPHIE

SHE COULDN'T BELIEVE it. Sacramento County was huge. There were more usable acres than Sophie could ever comprehend. Cole could work for any number of landowners, yet some act of unjust serendipity led him to the one patch of land that actually meant something to her.

Her eyes had welled with tears the moment he uttered the address. In truth, she always knew her setup was too good to be true. The McAllisters had let her rent the land for nearly a song. For the first year, they operated without a contract. Not even a handshake—just an understanding that Sophie would tuck her rent check into a lovely little bouquet settled neatly onto the McAllister's front porch the first of each month.

Sophie's father had prodded her to at least get the agreement in writing. For years, that was in the form of chicken scratch on a donut shop napkin. Last year, however, when Sophie took on more responsibilities with the Farmers' Market, she decided to get her legal ducks in

a row. She had a land lease drafted up and Kelly McAllister had gladly signed it, stating she couldn't even picture
the land anymore without Sophie's beautiful flowers
dotting it.

Apparently, at some point in the last 365 days, all that
had changed.

Sophie knew of the *Backyard and Beyond* competition.
In fact, her middle brother, Derek, covered it yearly for his
television station, interviewing the different landscape
architects throughout the duration of the event. Sophie
couldn't deny the beauty in many of the finished projects.
But she'd never heard of anyone hiring out of state talent
for the local event. She wondered if that was even allowed.
She'd have to consult the rulebook in hopes of discovering
some forgotten loophole. She'd do almost anything to keep
from having her rented soil torn up and landscaped by the
likes of Cole Blankenship.

She hadn't intended to come across as rude, but she
figured her silence conveyed only that. She just knew if
she opened her mouth to speak, her eyes would take that as
permission to open up the floodgates of emotion. She
wasn't typically a crier, but something about being caught
so unbelievably off-guard caused her to tear up and she
didn't want a complete stranger to see her in that state of
vulnerability. No, she would wait until she was by herself
before she let her emotions get the best of her.

And she did just that after she returned to her townhome, but not in the form of crying. She marched straight
into the kitchen, yanked the half-consumed carton of mint-
chocolate-chip from the freezer, and hunkered down on the
living room couch to eat her emotions instead.

The first spoonful took the edge off just a bit. The

second shaved off even more. By the third, Sophie no longer wanted to run Cole over with her truck. In fairness, she just wanted to bump him a little bit, not completely mow him down. By the time the carton of ice cream was entirely gone, Sophie felt much lighter, but that could've been the sugar rush contributing to her unnaturally euphoric state.

What would she do without her flowers? It wasn't as though she could just find another place to farm. She knew she had negotiated an incredibly favorable lease, a deal she wouldn't likely be able to strike up anywhere else. Could it all really be taken away so quickly, and without any say on her part?

She didn't have time to mull it over fully, as the day had gotten away from her and when she glanced at the clock, she startled to realize she had less than fifteen minutes to meet her newest clients for a wedding consultation. For a fleeting moment, she contemplated cancelling, but Sophie knew that throwing herself into her work was the only real way she'd be able to block out the afternoon's disappointing turn of events.

She gathered her binders, slung her purse over her shoulder, and jumped into the truck to head back into town. Other than her flower field, Heirloom Coffee was her favorite little spot in Fairvale. A high school friend had opened it years back, and Sophie loved supporting other small business owners wherever she could. The shop also displayed Sophie's flowers on their bar and tabletops, and Sophie knew many of her clients came to her through way of Heirloom Coffee.

Like most days, the shop was packed, so she had to circle the parking lot twice before a spot opened up. She hadn't accounted for those extra minutes, and her clients were already seated with their beverages in hand when she pushed open the coffee house door, the bell above chiming her tardy arrival.

"I'm so sorry!" Sophie said in a flurried rush as she unloaded her binder and books onto the café table. The young bride and groom-to-be stood to greet her. "I thought I gave myself enough time, but I always underestimate the parking situation here."

"No worries at all," Marie Connors said, leaning over the table for a hug. She smiled brightly. "We just got here. Go grab yourself something to drink. We're happy to wait."

Sophie glanced over to the barista bar, noticing a line several people deep. "No, it's fine. I'll get something later when there's a lull. Let's get started, shall we?"

❧

THERE WAS NOTHING more rewarding than hitting a project completely out of the park. Sophie had been in tune to her clients' requests, and she knew they would love her ideas for their late May wedding. She had talked to several of her flower farmer friends to make sure she could secure the varietals she had in mind, and once she knew it would be a go, she hit the ground running.

She watched the bride's eyes light up with each sketch she slipped across the table for approval. They had requested a rustic theme, and Sophie knew the Mason jar centerpieces, filled with asters, zinnias, and delicate Queen Anne's Lace filler would be right in line with their vision for the big day. She drew two possible renderings for the arbor planned for the altar, and she was so pleased when they chose the one with boughs of eucalyptus. It was the least expensive of the two options, but Sophie didn't care about that. It was never about money for her, even though the flower farm was her livelihood. She genuinely wanted her clients to have the wedding of their dreams. That she could be even a small part of sharing in that dream was payment enough. Unfortunately, though, she couldn't pay her bills in fulfilled dreams.

"I want to make sure you're still okay if I work with a few other farms to secure all the flowers and greenery we'll need," Sophie said as she wrapped up the meeting. "Everything will still be one-hundred-percent locally grown, but I don't currently have all of these specific flowers we discussed growing on my land." She paused, unable to stop herself before saying, "I'm not sure I'll have *anything* growing on my land, actually."

Marie's eyes went doe-wide. "What's happening with your flowers?"

Her fiancé, Peter, took ahold of his bride's hand, panic flashing across his face, too. "Is everything okay with the farm, Sophie?"

She waved them both off, though their concern was endearing. "I'm sorry. I shouldn't have even said anything. That was really unprofessional of me." She could feel those persistent tears creeping their way back into her eyes. She blinked rapidly. "I'm not even exactly sure what will end up happening, but apparently the McAllisters have decided to participate in the *Backyard and Beyond Summer Showcase* this year."

"And you think they'll take out your flowers?" Marie

gasped audibly. She clasped her chest. "That would be terrible!"

"I don't know what's going to happen, but I don't feel good about it."

"You do have a lease agreement, though, yes?" Peter asked. His brows tightened together and his statement came across equally scolding and concerned.

"I do, but I feel like it's already a done deal."

"Not if you have a signed contract. I'd be happy to take a look at it for you."

Sophie remembered that Peter had recently passed the bar, and though she was grateful for his offer, something about seeking legal advice made her stomach twist painfully with apprehension.

"As long as you have a signed lease, they can't just take the land from you. Not without a fight, at least."

Sophie wasn't up for fighting, and she certainly wasn't up for a legal battle. Expelling a breath, she looked over her shoulder, noticing the line had dwindled down over the course of their conversation. She sure could use a drink, if only a caffeinated one.

She hooked her thumb over her shoulder. "I'm going to go grab myself something real quick. Can I refresh anyone's cup while I'm at it?"

Both Marie and Peter waved her off, and the couple flipped through Sophie's sketches again while she gathered her wallet from inside her purse and slipped into line. She appreciated Peter's offer for help, but she couldn't let her thoughts travel down a road that led to the county court-house. No, she'd have to come up with a different way to solve this problem. Kelly McAllister was a reasonable person. Surely she could plan a brunch date with Kelly and the two could discuss just what this backyard remodel meant for the farm. Maybe there was a way for both to co-exist peacefully.

Stepping up in line, Sophie studied the decorative chalkboard listing seasonal drinks. While the lavender mocha had been her go-to in recent weeks, she couldn't resist the appeal of the vanilla rose latte which was the current featured drink on the sign. Sophie found it funny that even her preferred coffee beverages involved flowers in some way. She was nothing if not predictably consistent in her tastes.

"Hey you."

Startled by the sound, Sophie dropped her wallet and it clattered to the floor, coins spilling out like disoriented ants scurrying across the checkered tile. When she bent down to pick up her mess, the blue eyes peering out through black-framed glasses met hers for the second time that day.

"Cole!" she said, more of a gasp than a greeting. She scrambled to gather her belongings and her composure, failing to do either with any amount of distinguishable grace.

"Didn't think I'd get to see you again so quickly," Cole said, his mouth doing the same annoyingly charming upturn it did earlier when Sophie had tried so hard not to open hers to say goodbye. She knew more than just words would come out if she had. Twin dimples pressed into his cheeks and Sophie's gaze stuck there against her will. "I'm glad to run into you, because is it just me, or did we leave things a little weird back in the truck?"

"We left things just fine. Totally fine. Speaking of, I should probably get back to my clients." Sophie jumped out of line, making quick backward movements like she was doing the moonwalk across the coffee shop floor. She bumped into a nearby chair with her backside.

"But you haven't even ordered anything," Cole stammered. His features narrowed in confusion.

"I wasn't planning to!" she called back. She knew she wasn't making any sense, but she had to get out of the conversation.

Sophie flipped around, raced back to the table, and dropped into her chair like a sack of potatoes. Marie and Peter glanced up from the binder.

"You alright?" Marie tilted her head.

"Oh, I'm fine. Just ran into someone."

"Would that someone be the guy whose eyes haven't left you since you came back to the table?" Peter asked. He lifted his cup to his mouth and took a sip. "Because he's still looking at you."

Sophie covered her own eyes with her hands, hoping to hide, or better yet, disappear entirely. "Is he? Seriously?"

"Yep. Do you happen to know him?"

"Know him? Not really. The only thing I know about him is that he's the reason I might not have a flower season this year."

Marie's mouth fell open. "No way."

"Yes, way. Unless I can *find* a way to keep the showcase from happening. Or, at the very least, keep the McAllisters from participating in it."

With her back to the line, Sophie couldn't see him approaching, but the wide-eyes of her clients peering over her shoulder gave away Cole's proximity. She felt his looming presence at her back. Something about that made her insides quiver in discomfort.

"Since you got out of line so quickly and all, I figured I would get you something. Vanilla rose latte?" A cardboard cup lowered over her shoulder and into view. Sophie took the drink, albeit hesitantly. It frustrated her to no end that he had gotten her coffee order correct without even trying.

"Thank you," she offered, shrugging, though sincerity was completely absent from her tone.

"Hi, all," Cole said. He thrust his hand across the table and shoved his way into their meeting. "I'm Cole Blankenship, a new friend of Sophie's."

Well, if that wasn't incredibly presumptuous.

Peter rose to stand, pressing his tie to his stomach as he did so and offering up his free hand in a shake. "Nice to meet you, Cole. I'm Peter Niles, Sophie's lawyer."

Even behind his stylish glasses, Sophie could see Cole's eyes bulge, and that was deeply satisfying in the guiltiest way.

"Lawyer?"

"Yes, sir."

The two men mirrored one another, a silent standoff in the middle of the coffee shop. Marie smirked at Sophie, then tacked on a quick, but perceptible, wink.

"You in some sort of legal trouble, Soph?" Cole asked.

"It's Soph-*ie*." She settled her cardboard cup onto the table with enough force to send coffee droplets spraying through the small lid opening and onto her blouse. Grasping for a napkin, she dabbed at it quickly. "And no. Not yet, at least."

"Anything I can help with?"

Why this stranger—albeit a handsome one—was suddenly acting like a long-lost friend, Sophie couldn't figure. "Definitely not."

"Alright, well, I'm sorry to hear about your situation." Stepping back and bending in a slight bow, Cole retreated from the table. "I hope to run into you again soon." He made friendly eye contact with Sophie and her clients, not that they deserved it. The trio had been nothing but clipped in both tone and conduct. "Nice to meet you all."

For a fleeting moment, Sophie felt a twinge of remorse for snubbing Cole twice in one day—within one afternoon, no less. Surely he deserved the courtesy of a goodbye, but she couldn't muster the ability to utter one. She just wanted him gone.

"Okay, then," Cole said, maintaining his grin. "See you around." He saluted in a half-wave and made way for the door.

Once out of earshot, Sophie blew out a breath. "Ugh," she groaned, eyes rolling.

"I meant it when I said I'd be happy to take a look at your contract, Sophie," Peter offered once more. "But judging by the way he was looking at you, I think that man would be pretty easy for you to negotiate with all on your own. I get the idea he'd like to get to know you more, and I doubt he wants that to take place in a court of law."

That statement made Sophie's stomach flip, and she wasn't sure if it was out of flattery or disgust. Evidently, that was a very fine line when it came to Cole Blankenship.

4

COLE

"*I* WANT TO win at any and all costs," Kelly McAllister said. The statement sounded ludicrous, like it belonged coming out of the mouth of a corrupt businessman and not a middle-aged homemaker. "That's why we hired you. Your father and a dear friend of ours, Ralph Havertown, go way, way back and your firm comes highly recommended. If Ralph thinks you're the best, then you're the best in my book, as well."

"Good ol' Ralph." Cole nodded. He took another sip of his coffee, which had cooled to an unfavorable temperature. Still, it was one of the best lattes he'd ever had, and he was happy to discover a new go-to spot so quickly upon settling into town. Fairvale was feeling more and more like home already and that was an immense relief to Cole. "Ralph's practically my uncle. He and Dad were roommates back at Duke. I was even in Little League with his son before they moved to California. We're as close as you can get without being blood related."

"He mentioned something along those lines." Kelly

was nearly old enough to be Cole's mother, but it was obvious she'd taken meticulous care of her features over the years, likely utilizing the help of a surgeon's hand to maintain her beauty. Based on the large painting of the couple hanging over the mantle, Cole gathered that her husband, Theodore, likely cared less about his physical appearance and more about his economic status. Their home boasted a wealth that hinted at impeccable and expensive taste.

"Have you entered this competition before?" Cole inquired, wondering if a recent loss was the driving force behind Kelly's persistence upon winning.

"No," Kelly said as she drew her glass of chardonnay to her mouth. She left thick, red lip prints on the crystal rim, like a marker on paper. "In fact, we haven't really even touched the backyard the entire time we've lived here. Theodore did a lot of traveling these last few years, which has left little time for yard work. We've had an unspoken agreement throughout our marriage that the indoors is my domain, the outdoors, his responsibility. And since he wasn't really around to do anything with it, it just sort of sat there."

Cole looked around the home. He and Kelly had settled into the dining room to discuss the preliminaries, but from his vantage point, he had a sweeping overview of the downstairs in its entirety. Everything in its place, everything with a purpose. It was a home he'd be afraid to touch anything in, for fear he'd break something he couldn't afford to replace. It wasn't quite a museum, but bordered on that territory.

"You've done a lovely job, Kelly," he said, not out of obligational flattery. It truly was a beautiful home even if it wasn't in line with his particular tastes. "So for the outside, is there anything currently set up out there? Drip system? Weed barrier? Any landscaping of any kind?"

"How about we just take a look? I know you tried to stop by yesterday and couldn't get in. I apologize that I didn't leave the gate code for you ahead of time." Kelly threw back the last swallow of her wine and rose from the dining table. "Right this way."

Following Kelly McAllister through the kitchen, Cole quickened his stride to beat her to the large French doors. He reached out to hold them open for her.

She smiled her thank you and then flung her arms out wide with unexpected exaggeration once over the threshold. "Behold, Cole! Your canvas!"

Squinting into the sun which slanted in the sky, about to begin its slow slip into the horizon, Cole looked out over the plot of land, his brow shaded with his hand. Kelly wasn't kidding when she called it a canvas. It was an almost entirely blank one, at that. The only things he could see were parallel ruts running one-hundred feet long at the border of the property, around fifty or so if he were to venture a guess. Some had small green tufts dotted along the rows, but there was no established vegetation to speak of.

Kelly followed his gaze. "We rent that part out to a local flower farmer, but we can move it wherever we need to. I don't think she's done all that much this season yet, anyway. Maybe planted a few seeds, but hardly more than that."

Cole didn't like the idea of uprooting someone else's already established work, but the location of those rows would serve perfectly for the water feature he had in mind.

He could envision it all coming to life already, his ideas rising up out of the ground in three-dimensional form.

"I'm not sure that'll be necessary. We can likely work around it and it would still turn out just fine," he suggested.

"*Just fine* will not win the title of the *Backyard and Beyond Best.* That's the goal here, Cole, to win this year's competition. It's vital we do anything in our power to make sure that happens. We have some space along the north side of the house that the farmer can use. Our contract doesn't specify which portion of land she gets to work, just the overall size she can utilize. Anyway, I don't plan to renew her lease after this year, so it's really a moot point."

Something about the turn in their conversation didn't sit well with Cole, but he had been hired to do a job, and he had every intention of making sure it resulted in a happy client, and an even happier boss. This was his chance to prove to his father that the firm would be in good and capable hands once his dad's retirement rolled around.

"I saw the original sketches you sent over, Cole, and I know you're the man for the job. I'd love if you would spend some time over these next few days just expanding on those original drawings," Kelly said. "I'll give you the code to the back gate this time so you can come and go as you please. Feel free to spend as much time out here as you need. Then let's plan to reconnect early next week to see what you've come up with. Does all of that sound good to you?"

"Absolutely. Sounds like a great plan. Thank you for entrusting this space to me, Kelly. I won't let you down."

~

COLE PULLED HIS glasses from his face and settled them onto the tabletop. He rubbed vigorously at his eyes, pushing his fists into them and twisting there until he saw stars behind his eyelids. Staring at a computer screen for hours on end wasn't doing his already poor vision any favors, but it went with the territory.

He'd arrived at his short-term rental home just after sundown and quickly set up his laptop at the kitchen table, plugging it into the wall so he could begin. He had so many ideas floating around in his head regarding the McAllister project and he knew he needed to get them down on paper. Earlier that day, Kelly had sent over a plot map with the property dimensions and lines, which gave him the necessary information he needed. After a quick phone call to his dad just to make sure everything was a go, he set to work.

Cole had been at it for three hours when his stomach rumbled audibly. Once again, he'd worked straight through dinner. He didn't have plans to visit the car rental company until the next day, so instead he pulled up a web browser tab to order pizza delivery. It would have to be a night in. Rather than go with a chain, Cole opted to do a bit of research to find out which joints the locals preferred. After all, he had plans to stay in Fairvale for the next two months. While that wasn't enough time to become an actual resident, it was surely enough time to become deeply immersed in the town's culture.

Googling the Fairvale Chamber of Commerce, Cole clicked on the dining icon at the top of the page. There were several restaurants listed: Mexican, sushi, and a steakhouse called Buckeye Billy's. Scrolling down, Cole found the number for Ziggy's Zesty Pizza and picked up his cell phone to place an order for a medium Hawaiian. He knew he was in the minority, but he just couldn't resist fruit on his pizza. It reminded him of the last time they'd vacationed as a family in Maui—the final trip his older brother, Caleb, would ever go on.

It must've been a slow night in Fairvale, because it wasn't even twenty-five minutes later when the pizza delivery guy rapped on the door, his knock a loud percussion against the wood. Cole tipped him generously. He knew how hard it was to make an honest paycheck as a teenager. He'd always been lucky enough to work for his father, but something about that never felt as honest as it should. In a way, he envied the delivery kid with his go-getter attitude and the way he earned his own money without it being handed to him by a family member.

Cole was determined to *earn* his paycheck for the McAllister project. He would devote himself completely to its success over the next couple of months, and they would come out with a win. That was the only option.

Pulling a steaming slice of pizza from the cardboard box, Cole took a bite, savoring both it and the needed break from hunkered down work. His shoulders ached and he rolled them to work out the kinks of knotted muscle. He hadn't always been so tense, but he couldn't quite maintain the peace of his younger years when he didn't have the weight of responsibility bearing down on him. It wasn't as though he was old by any means—he'd only recently celebrated his thirtieth birthday—but with each passing year, he felt the increasing pressure of performance, this invisible weight that left him with a tightness he had to work hard to loosen.

With half the pizza gone, Cole felt instantly better, but he hadn't gained the energy he'd hoped to from the meal. Rather, he felt that lazy food coma settling in. He squinted at the clock hanging on the opposite wall. It was nearing ten o'clock, and with the three-hour time difference, his body thought it was the next day already. If he were wise, he'd shut his laptop and call it a night. But he wasn't wise, and it certainly wasn't wise to pull up the chamber website again, because when he clicked on the *Upcoming Events* tab, he saw Sophie Potters' grin smiling back at him through the computer screen.

His breath caught.

Reading the copy on the page, his mouth flipped into a grimace, unable to match that jovial smile that radiated from her photograph.

"Local flower farmer begins her fifth growing season and second year in charge of the Fairvale Farmers' Market," Cole read aloud. He scanned the article, but words like *rented plot of land* and *living her dream* and *flower farming phenomenon* jumped off the screen like a slap against his face.

Why hadn't she told him that the land was hers when she'd dropped him off at the McAllister's the day before? She had been so quick to speed away, practically dumping him at the gate. The gate he didn't even have the actual entry code to. Surely she'd had that code and would've been able to share that information with him, but for some reason, she chose to withhold it.

The strained interaction at the coffee shop suddenly made more sense. Sure, Cole didn't know Sophie all that well, but her curt tone had taken him aback. It was forced and unnatural. Now he saw it as her way of not only protecting herself, but her farm—and he didn't blame her one bit for it.

But the lawyer. That was an interesting component. Cole didn't figure he'd be the one wrapped up in any legal issues, necessarily. Those would likely take place between the McAllisters and Sophie. Still, the thought of a back-yard design contest turning into something that required a judge and jury seemed downright ridiculous.

Exiting out of the browser, Cole snapped his laptop shut. He wished he hadn't discovered this information about the land and the farm, although he knew it was only a matter of time before it came to light. It was obvious that Sophie was trying to avoid him, but she wouldn't be able to continue once they were working the same plot of land, side by side. She'd have to play nice; it was the only reasonable option.

5

SOPHIE

*T*HE SOIL WAS cold against Sophie's fingers. She had pushed the top layers of earth warmed by the morning sun aside and into a mound by her feet. She had accidently left her gardening gloves in the truck, but she was so eager to get her second succession of bachelor's buttons into the ground that she'd decided to make do without them. She actually didn't mind the dirt under her nails. It was the mark of a great morning, akin to a baker's apron dusted with flour after a productive day in the kitchen.

As she had hoped, the seeds Sophie had sown before her Seattle trip had already burst through the surface, their green shoots reaching skyward like the satisfying morning stretch that accompanied a good yawn. This was such a precious time in the garden, the beginnings of great things. It felt like a slow and steady warm up. Then—almost all at once—her plants would bloom, patches of flowers bursting in celebration among the rows like popped corn over a fire.

During her first few years, she'd grown impatient with

the waiting, the abundance of summer impossibly far off. But Sophie had learned that worthwhile things took time. These little plants taught her a lesson in patience that no textbook ever could, and she loved that the land had the ability to shape and mold her character along with offering her a source of income and purpose.

After she finished that morning's seeding, Sophie walked the rows. She noted in her journal the many small buds forming on the plants she placed into the ground after the last frost. Within days, these buttoned-up buds would unfurl, their petals gracefully falling open like a woman letting down her hair. Then Sophie would no longer be alone among the flowers. The hummingbirds and the bees would flit about, buzzing around her like musical notes in the air. She loved that the blossoming of a flower was like an invitation, summoning these friends back into her garden to share in summer's bounty.

Already, the anger Sophie had let take root began to slip away. When it came down to it, she wasn't sure who to be angry with, exactly, but Cole had presented himself at just the right time to endure the brunt of it. She knew that wasn't fair. He'd probably been hired for this position by the McAllisters. He wasn't the one forcing her off the land. In fact, up to that point, no one had told her she had to go anywhere. No one had even made mention of Sophie or her flowers. Not to her face, at least. She figured there was hushed talk that she was unaware of, but until someone brought their plans for that space to her attention, Sophie would continue to farm.

Slipping her earbuds into her ears, she cranked up her favorite gardening playlist. Even though she'd set up drip irrigation, several of her newly planted rows required overhead watering. Once they sprouted, she'd switch to underground, so as to avoid pesky problems like powdery mildew which could threaten to wipe out her entire crop. Grabbing the hose at the end of a row, she uncoiled it and bent down to twist the lever on. Water shot out of the spout with the force of a pressure washer. Somehow, that dial always got switched. Clicking it counterclockwise, Sophie adjusted the spray to a light mist and swept the hose over the rows, back and forth.

The monotonous motions ushered in the calm she so craved. It was like meditation: restful and restoring. She had almost finished watering all of the garden when the flow suddenly cut off. Turning around, Sophie noticed the tangled hose with a kink in the line. She whipped it up and down like a jump rope, but the stubborn knot stayed.

Sophie tugged one earbud from her ear and when she heard voices several yards away, she instantly jumped. She'd been so wrapped up in her own little world of flowers and melody, she hadn't noticed Kelly McAllister and Cole's presence in the yard.

It was clear that Cole, on the other hand, had been completely aware of Sophie. When their eyes connected, the smile he flashed looked like one he'd been saving just for her, like it was a relief to finally offer it her way.

Sophie made herself grin back.

That only lifted Cole's smile even higher onto his cheeks, and it forced those dimples deeper.

It annoyed Sophie that he had such a fantastic smile. It was much easier to dislike someone who didn't look so amazing simply being happy.

Still grinning, Cole shot his hand into the air in an elated wave.

Sophie waved back, but there was no enthusiasm in the exchange on her end. She shoved the earbud back into her ear and blasted her music even louder as she uncoiled the hose and continued watering.

Like the day before, she could sense Cole's presence without even turning around to confirm his nearness. She had watched Kelly retreat into the house earlier. Cole had stayed out in the backyard with his sketchpad, furiously running his pencil over the pages, his gaze alternating between the landscape and the notes in his hand. It struck Sophie that he was just as much in his element as she was, and that thought had her feeling a pang of guilt. Maybe he wasn't the bad guy she'd created him to be. After all, he was just doing his job.

"Hey, Soph." Cole's greeting was muted, the rush of water from the hose and the tunes echoing in her ears muffling his voice. "Hey there, Soph!" he said again, this time a near shout.

Pretending to ignore him was no longer an option. Sighing, she pulled out her headphones and shoved them into the kangaroo pouch of her sweatshirt containing her cell phone and keys.

"Soph-*ie*," she emphasized.

"Soph*ie*," Cole corrected. "Fancy meeting you here."

"Is it though?" Sophie asked. She wore her skepticism on her face in squinted eyes and tight lips.

Cole looked over his shoulder, surveying the grounds. "No, you're right. It's not fancy at all. It's quite dirty, actually. And I now see just what you mean about the whole compost in your hair thing." He lifted a hand toward Sophie's brow, about to brush the dirt from her bangs, but halted when she recoiled. "Sorry."

That he had to apologize made Sophie hot with guilt. "It's fine." She swatted at her hair with her own hand. "So. You're *the* landscape architect, huh?"

"No one's ever called me *the* landscape architect before. I like the sound of it."

"I wasn't intending for it to be a compliment," she retorted. She shut off and dropped the hose to the ground, then placed her hands into her sweatshirt pocket. "I meant you're *the* landscape architect who's about to force an end to my barely begun flower season."

Cole's brow drew together behind his glasses. "I don't see any reason for that, Sophie. I think we can both achieve our goals here."

"And tell me exactly what your goal is."

"To win the *Backyard and Beyond* contest. I think you know that."

"And at what cost?"

"I'm not exactly sure what it will cost the McAllisters yet. I'm still running those numbers."

Sophie's eyes rolled. "You know I'm not talking about the monetary cost, Cole. At what cost to me and my portion of the farm?"

She noticed Cole's swallow, how his Adam's apple strained in his neck.

"Like I said, I think we can all achieve our goals here," he spoke again, revealing nothing. "Listen, why don't you let me take you out for a cup of coffee and we can discuss things a bit more? I'd love to show you some of my drawings."

"I'm not interested in your drawings."

"Okay." Undeterred, Cole pressed on. "Then maybe we could just chat about your flowers. Kelly said it's a cut flower garden. I didn't realize all flowers weren't considered cut flowers."

"They're specific flowers used for bouquets. Ones that grow long stems," Sophie corrected.

"Gotcha. Which varieties?"

"Do you honestly care, Cole?" she spat. "Because I've got a lot of work to do here, and I don't really have time to shoot the breeze with you right now."

Cole dipped his head to search out her eyes. "But you'll have time later?"

"I didn't say that—"

"Like around, say, 5:30?"

"That's dinnertime."

"Great! I eat dinner, too. Let's kill two birds with one stone and eat our dinners together."

He wasn't giving up, and his persistence would be infuriating if not for the low flutter in her stomach that caught Sophie off guard each time Cole parted his lips to speak. It did something to her that made her feel like a silly schoolgirl again and she didn't know how to get rid of the unwanted sensation.

"Come on," he tried once more, nudging her with his elbow. "You have to eat. Why not do that with me?"

Sophie began forming a short list of the reasons why she didn't want to have dinner with Cole, but he stood there smiling expectantly and she couldn't force the rejection into words.

"Fine."

"Not as enthusiastic an acceptance as I had hoped for, but I'll take it." Cole beamed and tucked his notepad under his arm and pencil behind his ear. "When can I pick you up? 5:15?"

Sophie shook her head. "No, I'll meet you. There's an Italian place on Main. Aromatizzare. I can't be there until 6:00, though."

"That'll be great," Cole said, but Sophie noticed the slight disappointment her words elicited. "You sure I can't give you a ride? You know, you've given me one before and I finally have my own rental car. It's only fair that I return the favor."

"I don't need any favors, Cole. Just food, which I'll be paying for on my own." She forced the point home so no aspect of their evening could be construed as a date. "We can talk about your plans for the contest then."

"Can we talk about more than that?"

"We'll see," was all she offered.

~

"HOW DOES THIS look?"

"Gorgeous!" Caroline blurted. She slurped another mouthful of ice cream from her spoon. With her legs tucked up underneath her, Caroline practically bounced on Sophie's bed.

"Gorgeous?" Sophie groaned. "That won't work." Retreating to her closet, Sophie tugged off the simple black dress and tossed it to the floor on top of the pile of garments that Caroline had declared as either "stunning" or "spectacular."

Sophie pulled a black and white checkered blouse from its hanger and slipped her arms into it, intentionally buttoning up the front one button higher than she normally would. Taking a pair of dark denim jeans from the shelf, she yanked them on. She chose to finish off the look with a low, black heel. Not too formal, but not her typical gardening attire.

She took in her reflection in the full-length mirror and hoped this particular ensemble would suffice.

"Am I missing something here?" Caroline hollered from the bedroom. "Don't you *want* to look gorgeous? I mean, as far as I'm aware, it's a compliment, not an insult."

Sophie stepped out into the room. "This isn't a date, Care, and I don't want to give him the wrong idea."

"Well, you certainly do look nice—dare I say *beautiful*? I think it'll be hard for you to look anything but that, Soph. Who is this guy, anyway?"

"Remember the one who came by with my bag the other day?"

"Glasses?" Caroline perked up. "I mean, Glasses is what I've been calling him in my head when I think about him."

"You've been thinking about him?" Sophie asked.

"I haven't been *thinking* about him, thinking about him." Caroline wobbled her head back and forth. "Just, you know, I told Derek about him and how he brought your bag to the house and we've been calling him Glasses ever since. Just a little nickname we have for him. He seriously rocks those spectacles, Soph."

"You talked to my brother about him? What on earth would you have to talk about? You guys don't even know him." Sophie couldn't understand how a man Caroline had only met for a split second could somehow become the topic of conversation.

"Just that it was nice to see you interact with the male population again. It's good to see you back in the game. I don't know—there just seemed to be a little spark between you and Glasses—" Caroline cut herself short. "What's his actual name?"

"Cole," Sophie said through a frown. "His name is Cole. And there wasn't any spark. And I'm not back in any game. There is no game."

"Got it. No game." Caroline scraped her spoon against the carton, digging for the last bit of ice cream at the bottom. "So it's just a date, then?"

"This is not a date. It's a working dinner. Totally professional."

"Well, this outfit certainly looks professional."

Sophie's shoulders slouched. "Too professional?"

"I thought that's what you were going for!" Caroline flung her spoon into the air in exasperation. "I can't win!"

"I'm sorry." Sophie offered a smile in apology. "You're right." She waved her hands. "I don't know why I'm being so weird about this. I mean, Cole's a nice guy."

"That's great!"

"No, it's not. It's much easier to dislike people who aren't so inherently nice."

"And why do we need to dislike him?"

"Because my pocketbook sort of depends on it. If I don't have a flower season, I don't have a paycheck. And why? All so someone can win some silly backyard contest?"

"It's actually not all that silly, you know. Derek said this year's winner gets a spread in *The Fairvale Flyer* and a check for fifty grand. His news station is really playing it up. Doubling their amount of coverage and everything. It'll bring a lot of attention to Fairvale, way more than the past years' competitions."

That news made Sophie flushed with irritation. "Seriously? Why is everyone else so excited about this? Am I the only one who isn't?"

"Probably. It's pretty big for our little town. Might even drive more people to the Farmers' Market, too. I think it's a win-win all around."

"A win-win, huh? Then why do I feel like such a loser?"

Jumping up from her seated position, Caroline wrapped Sophie in a bear hug, the only kind she knew how to give. "You're not going to lose in this, Soph. Exposure is always a good thing, business-wise. For the market, for your flowers."

"I suppose so," Sophie relented. "I don't know. I don't know why I even agreed to go to dinner with him."

"Because as you said earlier, he's a nice guy. And it's just business."

"Right." Sophie nodded. "Just business," she said, but it felt like she was trying to convince herself more than Caroline at that point.

6

COLE

*H*E HAD ARRIVED a half hour early, even though GPS told him it would be less than a ten-minute drive. Even still, Cole didn't want to chance being late. The rental car company had outfitted him with a relatively new forest green hatchback which slipped easily into the vacant parallel space directly in front of the restaurant. He decided to stay in his car rather than wait in the lobby, choosing to flip through his drawings with the hope that Sophie would like to do the same over their dinner. He was proud of the work he'd completed so far. His vision was really starting to take shape.

In all honesty, Cole wanted Sophie's input. Yes, their goals were different for the land, but he believed they could achieve a mutually beneficial outcome. He just wasn't sure if Sophie wanted that. It felt like she'd given up before they had even started. This wasn't an all or nothing scenario—at least Cole didn't believe it to be one.

Looking out through the windshield, he caught sight of a couple dining just on the other side of the restaurant's large front window. Twinkle lights lined the frame, pulsing like a steady heartbeat. Based on the bashful looks exchanged between the two, Cole figured it was a first date. The young woman would periodically glance down at her hands, then look up through thick eyelashes at the man across the table. It was endearing and for a brief moment, Cole hoped his dinner with Sophie would have a similar tone. But she had been clear that was completely outside the realm of possibility.

When the clock on his dash flipped forward to 6:10, Cole made the decision to wait by the entrance rather than in his car. Hands shoved into his pockets, he scanned the street for Sophie's truck, knowing he would hear it before it came fully into view, that old engine rumbling loudly down the road. As predicted, within five minutes he made out the low hum of her GMC creeping along the street. He tried to catch her eye with a wave, but she was busy scanning the road for an open space. After three loops around the block, Sophie finally slipped into a recently vacated spot directly across from the restaurant. She exited the vehicle, looked each way, and then hurried across the street, her heels clicking against the pavement like horseshoes on a cobblestone path.

Out of breath, she stepped up onto the curb.

"You know, you could've avoided that intense parking spot search if you just let me pick you up," Cole teased. He bumped his shoulder into hers.

She remained rigid. "It's fine. It's always crowded around here. I'm used to it."

She really wasn't offering him anything.

"Alright. So...shall we?" He splayed out an arm,

twisting at the waist toward the historic building. "I called ahead and made a reservation."

"You didn't need to do that."

"Why? Because it makes it sound too much like a date?"

Sophie yanked her head back. "No, because I'm friends with the owner. He gets me right in every time."

Cole let a breath sputter between his lips, figuring it conveyed his frustration. If it had, Sophie didn't appear to notice as she grabbed the handle to the door and flung it wide open with determination. Cole trailed behind.

"Bella!" an older man with a manufactured Italian accent greeted. He rounded the podium and swept Sophie into an over-friendly embrace. "So lovely to see you tonight, my sweet. I was just telling the cooks that the market officially opens next week. I've already made a list of produce to buy. Please tell me the gentleman with the fresh herbs will be there again this year."

"Danny?" Sophie withdrew from the hug, but still clasped hands with the affectionate owner. "Absolutely! Just got his check for his booth in the mail today."

"You've done such a great job with the market, my sweet Sophie. It's so nice to see it succeed. You were just what this town needed, but of course you know that, don't you?"

Beaming, Sophie scrunched up her nose in a smile that showed she was uncomfortable with the compliment, but grateful for it all the same.

"Dining for one again tonight? I've got your usual table open if you'd like it. We have the fire going since it's a bit chillier than normal. You'll just love it."

Stepping forward, Cole interjected, "Table for two,

actually. I made a reservation. It should be under Cole Blankenship."

The man's eyes rounded. "Oh," he said, his tone more hushed. "I see," he uttered like there was some sort of scandal involved in that information. He withdrew two menus from the podium drawer and waved them like a fan against his face. "Right this way."

Sophie pursed her lips but then huffed out a short breath and followed the man.

"Will this do?" he asked after leading them to a secluded table against the back wall of the building. A tea light candle floated in a round vase placed in the center of the table. To the right, a colossal stone fireplace climbed toward the ceiling, and the heat from the roaring blaze within it could be felt from several feet away, like the radiating warmth of a campfire.

"I don't know," Sophie said, visibly uncomfortable with the undeniably cozy space. "Don't you think it might be a bit hot so close to the fire?" She turned to Cole.

"Nope." Cole grabbed the menus from the man and pulled out Sophie's chair, which she reluctantly lowered into after a labored pause. "This will be just perfect." He slid the chair back up to the table and rounded it to take his own seat.

Bowing, the man retreated toward the front of the restaurant, leaving Cole and Sophie alone.

"I'm starving." Cole opened the menu excitedly. He scanned the options. "Everything on here looks amazing. What's your usual?"

"I don't have one."

Cole lowered the menu several inches, searching Sophie out over its edge. "Seriously? You have your own table, but you don't have a regular order? Why do I find that hard to believe?"

Sophie lifted her menu higher to shield Cole's scrutinizing stare. "Not sure why you find it hard to believe."

"Listen." Cole let his menu drop to the table. "I get that you don't like that we'll be seeing so much of each other at the McAllister's, but it seems like I've upset you in some way, and I'm having a hard time pinpointing exactly why that might be. Have I done something to offend you, Sophie?"

Hiding behind her shield, Sophie shook her head, only offering a terse, "Nope," as her reply.

Several wordless minutes passed between them. The busser came by with water to fill their glasses, but Sophie didn't glance up from her menu, not even when the ice gathered at the spout and tumbled out of the pitcher all at once, causing a cascade of water to slosh over the cup and onto the table like a break in a levee.

"I'm so sorry," the young man said in a voice quivering from embarrassment.

"No worries, buddy," Cole offered. He dabbed at the soaked tablecloth with his napkin. "It's just water. No harm, no foul."

The busser scurried away and Cole leaned back to settle into his chair. He drew his water glass to his mouth and pulled in a long sip as he took in the surroundings. The restaurant was small and generic in its kitschy Italian décor, but it did have an inviting atmosphere which made it easy to see how one could quickly become a regular. The prices were modest and so far, the service was acceptable.

"The Lover's Special."

Cole choked on his water. "Excuse me?"

"I get the Lover's Special," Sophie repeated. She refused to make eye contact as she studied her menu like there would be a test at the end of their meal. "See? That's why I didn't want to tell you. Not only is it a goofy name, but it's an obscene amount of food."

Cole couldn't keep from chuckling, and that only produced a deep scowl on Sophie's lips.

"I shouldn't have told you," she groaned.

"No, no," Cole cut in. "It sounds amazing." He read the menu description aloud. "Lasagna, stuffed shells, *and* manicotti. Count me in. We'll share it."

"Share?" Sophie looked horrified. "I usually eat the leftovers the next day for my lunch."

"Well, I'm pretty hungry, so I doubt there will be any leftovers, but if you need lunch plans, I'm happy to make some with you."

Rolling her eyes, Sophie yanked the folded napkin from the table and threw it onto her lap. "I'll figure out my own lunch."

Cole placed his drinking glass onto the table and studied Sophie. It was obvious she'd cleaned herself up after her day in the flower fields. Gone was the dirt that had smudged her nose; the same dirt his fingers had itched to dust off. She'd swept her long hair into a loose knot at the base of her neck and even though she needed none, Cole could tell she'd applied a bit of blush to her cheeks and shadow to her eyes. All things someone would do to prepare for a date. Still, he tried not to read into the apparent effort she'd taken to get ready for their time together.

"Can I ask you a question?" Cole inquired after the waiter came back and took their order.

"If I said no, would it stop you?"

"Probably not," Cole admitted, and when Sophie's lips lifted into the faintest of smiles, he felt that small victory. "When I showed up on your doorstep and met you for the first time, you seemed like an entirely different person. Definitely not the same one sitting across from me now."

"How so?"

"Well, for starters, you were approachable," Cole admitted, shrugging. "Honestly, now I feel like I can't come near you with a ten-foot pole for fear that I'll do something to completely turn you off."

"Not a ten-foot pole. More like a ten-foot plot line."

"So that's what all of this is about, then?" Cole slumped back in his chair. "You're worried about the contest's impact on your flowers, aren't you?"

"Yeah, Cole, I am," she asserted. "I get that this is just another job for you, but this is my everything. These flowers are more than just my income. They're the realization of a lifelong dream."

"Would you be surprised to know this isn't just another job for me? It's *the* job, Sophie. I have so much riding on this. Do I want the McAllisters to be pleased with the outcome? Sure. Of course, I do. But I'm seeking someone else's approval here, and that's my real driving force."

"Whose approval would that be? Your boss's?"

"Bingo," Cole answered. "And in this case, my boss just so happens to be my dad."

At that moment, the busboy came by with a basket of garlic bread, and when he settled it between them on the table, both Cole and Sophie reached out for a piece at the same time. Their fingertips brushed. Eyes wide, Sophie yanked her hand back like she'd been shocked.

"Sorry." Cole nudged his chin toward the basket. "You go ahead."

Sophie lifted the fabric liner and reached in for a piece. She held the bread up to her mouth. "Look. I know I've come across like I'm angry with you, Cole. I'm just frustrated with the situation, I suppose. This wasn't in my plans for the season. I'm still trying to wrap my head around it all. It's a lot to take in."

"That's understandable. You've had sole access to the land for several years now and here I come and threaten to change all of that. I get it. But I think if you would just take a look at my preliminary drawings, you'd see I don't intend to squeeze you out, Sophie. In my book, we have complementary strengths and I think we can ultimately work together to create something really beautiful."

For the first time all night, there was a palpable shift in Sophie's demeanor. That hardened edge softened, even if only slightly, and Cole saw it as a gift.

"Did you bring them with you?"

"My drawings?" Cole wiped his mouth with the napkin. "Yeah, I did. They're just out in the car, but I can go grab them—"

"No." She cut him off. "We can look at them after dinner. But I would like to see them."

She'd stressed that this would be a professional dinner only, but that statement offered the shred of hope that it could possibly mean something more. Cole wasn't sure why he grasped onto that hope, but it sure felt good to do so.

"You work for your dad?" she asked. "I take it you're close with your family, then?"

"Yeah, I work for him back home in Nashville. Five years now. I'm the junior landscape architect at his firm."

"And you have siblings?"

"A twin sister, Trista." He didn't mention Caleb, but he rarely talked about him, certainly not when he was just getting to know someone. "My parents are divorced and I'm not as close with them as I used to be, but that might have something to do with my dad being my boss and all. Changes the structure of a relationship, you know?"

Sophie nodded while she chewed. "I completely get that. My brothers used to be business partners, and as a result, they haven't spoken in years. Things can go south pretty quickly when you mix family and finances."

"What about you? Fernando back there said something about the Farmers' Market? You're involved in that?"

"This will be my second year running it. I bring out my flower bouquets and have a little table where I sell them, but my main job is to make sure the market runs smoothly. There's been a huge response from the community. All positive. I think people are tired of shopping for their food in a supermarket, you know? They like to know where it comes from. No middle man. Plus, there's nothing like purchasing fruit that was still hanging on the tree that very morning. Can't get any fresher than that."

"I like this."

"What?" Panic crept into Sophie's gaze. "What do you like?"

"Listening to you talk about your passions. You light up."

"I get more excited than I probably should about these sorts of things. If you haven't noticed yet," she said, sarcasm thick in her tone, "I tend to have big swings of emotion."

"*No*," Cole said, volleying the sarcasm right back. "Haven't noticed one bit."

"In fairness, I am like thirty percent Italian or something along those lines, so it goes with the territory."

"So you're about as Italian as your good friend, Fernando?"

"Oh, Fernando? He's one-hundred percent Armenian. That accent's completely fake."

"Yeah, I picked up on that," Cole said, laughing.

They continued their banter throughout dinner, and Cole was pleased that they were able to maintain a cordial tone for the remainder of the evening. He wasn't sure how long it would last, but he would enjoy it while it did. But what he enjoyed almost more than the conversation was the food. The Lover's Special was a real winner. They'd divvied up the portions, splitting everything onto two plates of equal size. Sophie hadn't been exaggerating—she really did love a good meal. She just dove right in and there was something refreshing about watching a woman eat without any worry as to how she came across. Cole had dated too many women in the past that would pick at their salad, just pushing lettuce around their plate with their fork like they were creating a mosaic out of their food. It was such a waste of a good meal, and a good paycheck.

Several times throughout their night, Cole would say something that would cause Sophie to burst into a fit of laughter and each time it caught him off guard in the best way, even when water sprayed out of her mouth during a particularly boisterous laugh. She'd apologized profusely, but if anyone needed to offer an apology, it was Cole. He'd told Sophie that he would keep their dinner strictly professional, but as their evening progressed, he realized at some point it had shifted from a formal meeting to something more. There was no denying their chemistry. It was clear in the way Sophie looked at him with rapt attention when he spoke about how he'd acquired his GMC as a teenager and it was evident in the way she let him take the bill from the waiter without a challenge.

"This place is a real winner, Soph," Cole said, catching himself. "Soph-*ie.*"

"You can call me Soph," she said as she gathered her purse from the back of her chair and unzipped it. She reached in and took out a tube of peach-colored lip gloss and ran it across her mouth. "Since we've sort of had our first date and all."

Cole perked up like a dog being told it was time for a walk. "Oh really? Is that what this was after all? A date?"

"Well, I mean, you did pay for my meal."

"Correction. I paid for *my* meal. You just ate half of it."

Sophie smiled and tucked her gloss back into her purse. "I would've eaten a lot more if you hadn't hogged all the manicotti. You took the two biggest pieces!"

"Really? I didn't even notice. I suppose we'll just have to come back here again so you can get your fair share."

"Nah, next time I'm taking you to One Fish, Two Fish."

"Next time?" Cole's eyebrows shot up. "We're getting dinner number two on the books already?"

"Only because you strike me as the sort of guy who's never had sushi and I want to be with you for that adventure," Sophie said, shrugging noncommittally. "But in all honesty, Cole, we probably shouldn't make a habit of this."

Cole's throat tightened with a swallow, the high he'd been riding throughout their evening suddenly crashing like a rug tugged out from underneath him. "We shouldn't?"

"My brother works for Channel 12 News."

"And that's a problem because?"

"Because they sponsor the *Backyard and Beyond Summer Showcase.* It's sort of a conflict of interest for us to be involved."

A word never sounded so enticing to Cole. "Involved?"

"Well, you know what I mean," she stammered, but he didn't know. "It's just—I'm not saying we're anything or that this is anything or even the start of anything." She waved her hand between them. "I can't be connected to you since my brother works for the station, Cole. It would jeopardize everything. Two years ago, the first place winner had their title stripped when it was discovered the contestant was second cousins with one of the camera guys. The station seems to take things very seriously when it comes to contest rules."

Cole dropped his napkin to his lap. "Well, that stinks."

"I probably should've brought that up earlier. I'm sorry."

"It's not your fault." Cole shrugged, hoping to hide his disappointment, but he doubted he did a decent job. He smiled when he joked, "Any chance we can get your brother to quit his job? I mean, he's not really committed to being an anchorman, is he? What was his back up plan if this career choice didn't work out?"

"This *was* his backup plan after the failed startup business with our brother. But you can ask him yourself on Sunday if you like. We have a family dinner at my parents' house and you're welcome to tag along—but only as an acquaintance I barely know," she said, winking.

How this 'strictly business dinner' had not only turned into a date, but into an invitation to meet Sophie's parents, Cole couldn't comprehend, but he didn't question it. "I'm happy to pretend to be someone you drug in off the street. And believe it or not, I'm actually dying for a decent home cooked meal."

"Well, that's kind of ironic because my mom's cooking just might kill you."

"Man, if that's the case, I think I should cash in our sushi trip before I kick the bucket."

Grinning demurely, Sophie's lips bent into a smile. "Fair enough. Tomorrow at noon." Looking up at him in a way that made Cole's breath catch, she said, "And this time I will take you up on that offer for a ride."

7

SOPHIE

*W*HAT ON EARTH had she been thinking? That was the question that looped in Sophie's brain throughout a fitful night's sleep, like an annoying cycle of déjà vu. She knew it wasn't a good idea to let her guard down with Cole, yet somehow she'd done exactly that the night before at the restaurant. Not only had she let it down, she'd invited him completely in—to her parents' house, no less! Was she that starved for attention from a man that she would so unabashedly throw herself at the first eligible one to so much as glance her way?

There was an embarrassment that tainted the memories from their dinner that she couldn't shake, and she knew she was solely to blame for it. Why did she assume Cole would be interested in exploring any sort of relationship other than a strictly professional one? When she brought up the conflict of interest scenario involving her brother, she'd truly overstepped. It felt foolish to think that just because Cole was nice and that they mutually enjoyed one another's company that anything would progress beyond a short-lived friendship.

Cole was in California for two months, after which he would go back to Tennessee and continue working at his father's firm. Sophie would stay in California. Why she felt the need—or desire—to foster any relationship other than one of being mere acquaintances made no sense.

After wrestling with these thoughts all night long, Sophie rose well before her alarm and shut it off before it had the chance to do its job. Slipping out from under the covers, she swung her legs over the side of the mattress to let her feet dangle. She was due for a pedicure, but always felt embarrassed when she went in for the first one after the long winter season, her feet calloused and neglected. She just wasn't a manicured sort of woman and likely never would be. While she'd forced her feet into heels the night before, she was much more comfortable in a pair of muck boots or garden shoes. She doubted many men were attracted to that, but she couldn't help but notice the way Cole had looked at her the night before. There was a spark just behind those glasses, his eyes bright with interest, hanging on each word of their conversation like he truly wanted to gain something from it.

Maybe that captivated attentiveness had to do with their lines of work. There was obviously quite a bit of overlap there. While Cole's knowledge of plant life was just as extensive as hers, he appreciated certain varietals for their drought tolerance or reasonable price tag while Sophie cared more about how a particular flower would look when coupled with others in a market bouquet. But still, they understood one another, spoke the same language, and reciprocated an equal passion.

Of course they would hit it off. It made sense. But it bothered Sophie that she had been so forward, so bold. And she felt stupid for bringing up the whole bit about her brother. There was no need to even mention that. There were so many degrees of separation between Derek and Cole that it didn't even matter.

Yawning, Sophie went to her closet to retrieve her bunny slippers and yellow terrycloth bathrobe. She didn't have plans to go to the farm that morning and instead intended to spend her hours with her journal, going over her last season to gauge if she was on the right track with this new planting. The previous year had been the most prosperous one yet—the true benchmark of her success. If she followed closely to last year's strategy, she figured she'd be in great shape.

As Sophie shuffled through the house toward the kitchen, her slippers collected an alarming amount of dust. The home was well past due for a deep cleaning, but with both women working hard to pursue their dreams, household chores often fell by the wayside. Eventually, someone would drag out the vacuum or swipe a rag over the kitchen tile, but having a neat and tidy townhome was not at the top of either woman's list of priorities.

But the thought of bringing a man into her home in this current state of disarray had Sophie reaching for the linen closet to pull out the feather duster and spray. It wasn't like she would invite him to stay long, but she had agreed to let Cole pick her up. Even if he so much as glanced over her shoulder and into the house, he would likely be shocked by what he saw.

So she set to it, and after a frenzied morning of housework that had completely gotten away from her, Sophie was horrified by what *she* saw when her gaze caught her reflection in the oval mirror above the piano. Wild hair sprung out in every direction from her head like Medusa's tangle of snakes. Her mascara, which she hadn't wiped clean the night before, was smudged all over her eyelids like two black eyes. Now that the house was sufficiently cleaned, Sophie had to get herself cleaned up, too.

Just as she spun on her heel to retreat to the bathroom, an unexpected knock on the door nearly shot her through the roof. Eyes wild, she searched for the clock on the wall. It read just after eleven, but now that Sophie thought on it, that was the exact time it had showed an hour earlier when she'd glanced at it. Could it be that the hands hadn't budged at all during the time that had lapsed?

Another knock on the door—this one louder—had Sophie's blood pressure rising sky high.

"Sophie? You in there?" Cole's low baritone echoed through the door.

"Oh no. No, no, no." Like a cat on a Roomba, Sophie spun in disoriented circles. "Just a minute!" she yelled, but she had no real plans for that minute other than to continue to spiral out of control.

"We did say today, right?" Cole spoke through the slip of space between the door and the frame.

"Yep! Today!" Sophie hollered. Frantic, she reached into the hall closet and grabbed her winter coat, flipping the hood up and tugging the drawstrings tightly around her face to cover her unruly hair. She swiped at her cheeks with the back of her hand and pulled on the front door handle, not at all surprised to see Cole's eyes widen briefly before he recovered with all the controlled finesse Sophie lacked in the moment.

"Hey," he said, but his voice was an octave higher than usual. "You ready to go?"

"Oh, yeah," she said. "Absolutely. Just give me a second."

Cole squinted. "Listen, it's okay if you forgot."

"I didn't forget," Sophie stammered. "The morning just got away from me. House cleaning and all."

Cole peered over the top of Sophie's head and into the home. "Looks great."

"It might, but I don't."

"I didn't say that at all. You look very..." He paused, proceeding with extreme caution. "*Creative.*"

Sophie looked down at her slipper clad feet, at her fuzzy robe cinched around her body and the army green coat she'd thrown over the ridiculous ensemble. She roared out a laugh. "I'm so sorry, Cole. I thought I was keeping an eye on the time, but today is the day the battery decided to give out on the old clock there," she explained. "In fairness, it's probably been out a week or more. I'm not big on details, apparently."

"And I'm not in a big hurry, so how about this? Why don't you go take a shower and get ready while I run over to One Fish, Two Fish and order us some take-out. By the time I get back, you should feel like a new woman." He caught himself. "Not that you need to. I actually like this whole comfort meets extreme warmth vibe you have going on here."

"No, you're right. I *do* need to feel like a new woman. Or anything other than the hugely embarrassed one I am at the present moment."

"No need to be embarrassed, Soph," Cole said with an

intentional wink that sent a jolt of awareness down Sophie's spine. "I think it's adorable."

It was as though *adorable* was the only word left in the English language, because it was all Sophie could hear playing in her head throughout her shower. That Cole found any shred of Sophie even the smallest bit attractive was utterly unfathomable, but he sounded so sincere that she had to choose to believe there was honesty intended in his words. Sophie had to chuckle as she remembered the great lengths she'd gone to the night before to make sure her appearance was nothing but professional. And here she was, looking like a cat lady preparing for the storm of the century, and somehow Cole found even that mildly appealing.

Something was off with this man, that was the only plausible explanation.

Since her previous outfits had unintentionally missed the mark, Sophie spent little time choosing today's attire, figuring it made no real difference, anyway. She threw on a loose, scooped neck white t-shirt that read *Support Your Local Farmer* in cursive across the front and slipped into her favorite boyfriend cut jeans that had holes worn in the knees and fraying pant hems. She was going for comfort, but not quite as much comfort as she had showcased earlier.

When Cole returned and knocked on the door, Sophie answered it with much less hesitation now that she felt moderately presentable. Plus, her stomach was eager to dive into that lunch. Without meaning to, she'd cleaned all the way through breakfast.

"I had no idea what to order, so I got a little bit of everything." Cole held the large plastic to-go bag up by his face and grinned. "Did you know they have a Fairvale Roll? Must be a pretty incredible town if they named a sushi roll after it."

"Oh! That one's my favorite!" She yanked the bag from his grip, then recoiled. "I'll share though."

"It's all yours. I ordered plenty."

Cole wasn't kidding, he had ordered more than two people could possibly eat in one sitting. In Sophie's flurry of cleaning, she'd missed the kitchen table, the plates and dishes from a dinner shared between Caroline and Derek the night before still resting on the tabletop. Rather than waste any more time, Cole and Sophie set up their meal on the coffee table. Sophie grabbed a throw pillow from the couch to sit on and tossed another Cole's direction. He caught it like a football against his stomach and smiled. It was sure easy to hang out with Cole now that Sophie actually gave herself permission to. Almost overnight, he had become a friend and no longer a competitor. That made all the difference in the world.

Just as she suspected, Cole was a sushi newbie. But rather than order chicken teriyaki, he seized the opportunity to try something new. He'd ordered multiple rolls, nigiri, sashimi—you name it. The coffee table had become a delectable rainbow of fresh fish cuisine.

Sophie grabbed two pairs of chopsticks from the bag and opened one, snapping the sticks apart with her hands. She passed the other set to Cole.

"You mind if I grab a fork? Point me in the direction of the cutlery drawer?" he asked, about to stand.

"You're going to eat sushi with a fork? That's almost blasphemous. Sorry, Cole, but you have to use chopsticks to really get the full experience."

"And what if I don't know how to use them?"

Sophie's mouth popped open like the very fish on the table. "You're teasing."

"No, I'm totally serious."

For some reason, that took her by complete surprise. Cole seemed like such a capable man. Chopstick holding certainly didn't seem like something that would throw him for a loop.

"Hmm." He frowned as he pulled the sticks from the paper sleeve. "Looks like I only got one anyway." He shrugged. "Guess I'll just have to use a fork."

"You need to pull them apart, silly." Sophie waved at him. "Here, give them to me." Taking the chopsticks from Cole, she split them at the seam and offered them back.

Cole looked at Sophie like she had just handed him a scrambled Rubik's cube. He managed to tangle each finger around the two sticks, like he was knitting a detailed sweater pattern.

Sophie pursed her lips, eyebrows furrowing. It was almost painful to watch him struggle. "Let me guess, you were the kid that needed to use those pencil grippers in order to hold your pencil correctly back in elementary school, right?"

"Hey, don't make fun. Those grippers were awesome."

"I know they were. I had an entire collection in my pencil box. Took my teachers until third grade to finally figure out I was actually left handed and didn't just have really terrible penmanship. So I'm not going to make *too* much fun of you for not getting this whole chopstick thing down."

"How very kind of you," Cole said at the same moment both sticks clattered to the table.

Rolling her eyes and laughing, Sophie grabbed ahold of Cole's wrist. She gathered the discarded chopsticks and placed them back into his hand, pulling apart his thumb and index fingers to slide them into the correct holding position. She tried to ignore the pulse she could feel in her wrist and hoped Cole would do the same. So she didn't have to stretch awkwardly over the coffee table, she got up on her knees and scooted closer.

"Like this," she said, working hard to keep her voice steady. She moved her hand over the top of his large one and mimicked the motion of opening and closing the chopsticks in his grip. "Got it?" she asked almost breathlessly. "What do you think?"

Cole's bright eyes locked with hers, their close proximity making his gaze all the more intense. She could feel his stare in every single one of her senses. "What do I think? Or what am I thinking? Because they're two entirely different things."

Sophie swallowed around the lump in her throat. "What are you thinking?" she murmured.

"I'm wracking my brain, trying to make a list of all of the other things I'm terrible at so you can teach me how to do those, too," he said, one eyebrow quirked up and his mouth edging into a mischievous grin.

Sophie blew out her trapped breath. She swiped at her bangs nervously and rocked back on her heels. "Okay, now you give it a shot all by yourself."

It didn't appear that chopstick proficiency was anything Cole would be adding to his résumé anytime soon, but he did give it a valiant effort. Sophie watched him struggle for a solid ten minutes before she reluctantly headed to the kitchen to retrieve a fork. It didn't seem fair that she was the only one enjoying their food so far.

"No way." He shook her off when she extended the offering. "You said I had to use chopsticks to get the full experience. I want the full experience." Taking just one stick, he stabbed at a piece of raw salmon draped over a clump of rice and then popped it into his mouth. He beamed a huge, closed-lip smile. "Delicious!"

"I know, right?" Sophie responded enthusiastically. She was so pleased that he liked it.

"No." Taking a napkin, Cole covered his mouth and spit into it. "I'm sorry, Soph, but that's totally disgusting."

"Maybe raw isn't the best first choice." She scanned the smorgasbord of food before them. "You have to start with something pretty harmless, like the California roll."

"By calling that one harmless, you are implying the others are harm*ful*. Why would I want to eat something that can harm me? No thank you, very much."

Sophie swatted at his chest and startled when Cole reached out and caught her hand. His dimples sunk into his cheeks with a massive grin. For a fleeting moment, he held her hand in his before releasing it.

"Okay," Cole said on a breath, "so the California roll is harmless. What else?"

Sophie's words took longer to form than usual, her stuttering brain misfiring all over the place. "The Fairvale's a good choice. Just deep fried shrimp, rice, and avocado."

Cole tilted his head and looked sideways at the roll in question. "What are all of those little orange thingies on top?"

"Tabiko."

He used his single chopstick to harpoon a slice of the roll and brought it up to eye level in examination. "Ta-bi-ko," Cole repeated, then it disappeared into his mouth in one large bite.

Sophie smirked. "Fish eggs."

Cole didn't even wait for the napkin this time before spitting out the contents of his mouth. "Seriously? How could you lead me so far astray?" He wiped his lips vigorously, then stuck out his tongue to swipe a napkin across it, too.

"You're being just a touch dramatic, don't you think?"

"Dramatic is not the word I would use. Adventurous. Spontaneous. Thrill-seeking. Those are all fitting descriptors."

"And what word would you use to describe your first sushi experience in general?" Sophie asked, enjoying their easy banter.

"I'd break it down into categories." Cole lifted a finger, ticking them off one by one. "The ambiance: clean and comfortable. The food: questionable. The company: pr—"

"Priceless," Sophie interrupted gleefully.

"I was about to say presumptuous, but okay." He recoiled as he spoke the words, anticipating the blow she dealt to his shoulder. "But in all seriousness, we should do this again. Next time, let's actually cook our food."

"I think next time my mom is the one doing the cooking. Hate to break it to you, Cole, but you'll be wishing for sushi at that point. Even tobiko."

8

COLE

$\mathcal{C}$ALIFORNIA MORNINGS QUICKLY became Cole's favorite time of day. The chattering of squirrels racing around a tree, a chase that swirled up the trunk like the coiled pattern of a barbershop pole, stood in such stark contrast to his usual view back at his father's Nashville office. Buildings rather than trees surrounded their workplace, like a forest forged from concrete. Sure, it only took a short drive to the countryside where he could take in a similar scene, but Cole's roots were in the city, even if they were in the form of cement footings and foundation.

At times it seemed strange that a firm responsible for creating landscapes would be located in the middle of the city, but every business needed a home base and Nashville was the ideal spot. Plus, it served as a great central location, with most of their clients just a short drive from town in either direction.

But in California, Cole had unofficially made Heirloom Coffee his office, mostly for the large outdoor seating offered to its customers. He loved the expansive teak decking that wrapped around a looming Heritage oak, like the tree was a purposeful part of the design and not just an element to work around. He greatly admired the intentionality of it.

For the past several mornings, Cole would order his iced Americano and banana bran muffin, and then spend the next few hours on the patio with his laptop open, the McAllister design pulled up on the computer screen. He'd not-so-accidently drop a few crumbs for his squirrel and bird friends to enjoy, all while basking under the invitingly warm California sun.

While he was doing just that, his phone buzzed across the table, rattling on the metal surface. He flipped it over and his stomach did a similar flip when he saw the caller ID. Cole swiped his thumb across the screen.

"Morning, Dad," he said. His throat felt tight with a lump he couldn't swallow.

"Hello, Cole," Martin answered. "I just thought I'd see how things were going with the project." His dad's voice was gruff and authoritative and it bothered Cole how easily it intimidated him. It always had. "I told the McAllisters I'd check in with you periodically—you know, just to be sure things are staying the course."

"All is well, Dad. In fact, I've got an interview in a few minutes, so I probably shouldn't be on the phone when he gets here. Mind if I call you back a little later?"

This particular morning, Cole had an interview planned with a potential landscape contractor for the project. While Cole was certified on the design end of things, he was rarely the one to do the actual labor. It was usually better that way because while he had a strong eye for design, delegation and execution weren't his specialty. The creative process was his wheelhouse. He could almost effortlessly visualize things that weren't there, bring into existence something that had yet to be imagined. But running and managing a crew of workers? He wouldn't even know where to start. He definitely needed a partner in that area.

"Who are you interviewing?"

"Just a possible contractor to help me run things at the property."

The notable pause in conversation let Cole know exactly how his father felt about that. "Help you run things? Or *run* things? There's a difference, Cole, and while I know you excel at design, you really need to analyze whether or not you are the best fit to be a part of the labor side of things."

Cole knew he wanted a bigger hand in the installation this go round. He wasn't sure if it was the fact that Sophie would be working the same land that ignited this desire to see this design through, start to finish, or if the contest had him feeling the pressure to be more intricately involved. More than likely, it was the hard-won approval of his father that was the real driving force. And comments like his father's previous one only made him more determined.

"Listen, Dad, I really should go. Things are great here. You can pass that along to the McAllisters. Talk to you later."

Without meaning to, Cole clicked to hang up before his father uttered his goodbye. He thought about calling back, but they didn't have that type of relationship, one where they admitted their wrongs or offered apologies.

Cole knew he wasn't the favorite child, and he was okay with that. It was a reality he'd settled up with way back in his youth when he'd chosen sports over education. Though his father never verbally indicated his disappointment, the fact that Martin had directed every conversation involving the future of the family business to Cole's older brother, Caleb, more than hinted at the fact that he had placed all his work hopes and dreams upon his eldest son's shoulders.

When Caleb died unexpectedly in an accident on a family vacation, their father nearly collapsed under the weight of grief. He didn't say it at the time, but Cole knew his dad also experienced anxiety over Blankenship Backyard Design's future.

It was then that Cole knew he had to take an extreme turn on his own life path. He rejected his full ride, out-of-state football scholarship and instead enrolled in a local college so he could stay closer to home and learn under his father's tutelage. Even still, he never felt like second best. Cole and Caleb were vastly different people, any sort of real comparison difficult to come by. Not that Martin favored Caleb for any envious reasons. It was merely the fact that the father and son had similar minds and interests, and as a result, spent much more time at the office together.

Cole knew with time his father would be able to shift those business dreams over. He just had to prove himself. Making sure Cole had the right team in place for the McAllister project was the first step, and after ten minutes into his meeting with Tanner Lightly, Cole knew he'd found his man. Tanner was young, likely fresh out of college, and had that eager hunger evident in his eyes and speech. The entire time Cole showed Tanner his initial 3-D renderings, Tanner's head remained in a constant nod of agreement, like a bobble head upon his shoulders.

"That pergola," Tanner said, pointing to the image pulled up on the screen, "I managed a crew of guys that built one almost identical to it last fall. Not too far from here, actually—maybe five miles or so up the road if you'd like to check it out."

"Definitely. That would be awesome," Cole replied, grateful for the suggestion. "I'm a little worried with the size of the structure that the boards might start to warp and twist if we keep them the length I drew them."

"That's not a problem at all. We can brace it here and here." Tanner drew two imaginary loops with his finger on the computer screen. "And if the homeowners are open to it, we can use manufactured rather than real wood. That might help with the potential warping issues."

"They might be open to it, but honestly, I'd really like to keep all elements as natural as we can. My main objective with this particular design is to give it a rustic, earthy feel. I want raw woods, natural stones, native plants."

Tanner continued with his encouraging nod. "There's a great nursery here in town that has an entire section devoted to California horticulture. It's my go-to plant store for all of my local projects. We could swing by this afternoon if you've got time." Tanner caught himself. "That is, if you think I'm the right man for the job."

"Tanner, I think you might be an even better fit for this job than I am."

"Not a chance." Tanner threw back a swallow from his

coffee cup and placed it back onto the table between them. "I have absolutely no clue how to design any of this, much less use the computer programs necessary to create something on this scale. I can swing a hammer and dig a hole and rally a crew, but I need someone else to provide the inspiration."

Cole beamed, feeling confident that this first interview would be the only one necessary. It baffled him how everything in Fairvale had so easily clicked into place.

"I think we'll make the perfect team." He shot his hand out for a shake. "Welcome aboard, Tanner."

∼

SOPHIE PULLED INTO the parking space directly next to Cole, but hadn't realized it yet. Cole stole that opportunity to admire her while she got out a compact from her purse and regarded her reflection, rubbing her lips together like she'd just applied gloss to them. Cole couldn't help but find it endearing. In reality, there was no need for any of it. Sophie looked flawless to him in the way that true, natural beauty needed no enhancement.

Lightly tapping his horn, he drew her attention. She jumped, then flashed a wide, toothy grin when she saw Cole seated in the car beside her. Cole unbuckled his seatbelt and stepped out from his vehicle.

"Long time, no see," Sophie teased as she hopped down from her truck and rounded it to greet Cole. For a brief moment, she halted, as though unsure how they should greet one another. Cole got it. He didn't know how to, either. It had only been a few days, but they were past the formal handshake portion of their relationship. Even still, he felt wrong in assuming she'd be okay with a hug, so instead he did the whole awkward side-hug thing like he was still in junior high. Sophie stammered in her steps, but leaned into Cole's side, her hand hooked up on his shoulder, squeezing it lightly.

"Thanks for agreeing to meet us out here, Sophie. I thought it might be good to have your eye when selecting our plants for the project. I'd love to pick out ones that will compliment your garden to make sure it all really flows. That's the ultimate goal here: to make it one seamless landscape."

"I appreciate that. I think the main thing we need to keep in mind is that my garden is ever changing—the sizes of the plants, the colors, the overall amount depending on harvest times and such. For the backyard, you might want to focus on slow-growing shrubbery that will maintain the consistency that my flower field lacks."

If talking about plants could be a turn on, this conversation was just that for Cole. He chuckled to himself.

"What?" Sophie's brow furrowed. "Did I say something funny?"

"No." Cole shook his head, grinning. "It's just that you totally get it. It's beyond refreshing."

A car door slammed near them and Cole swung his gaze toward the direction of the sound. It was Tanner, exiting a shiny, black SUV and crossing the lot to come over to them, a notebook tucked under his arm and aviator glasses perched on his nose like he was about to audition for a role in Top Gun.

"Hey man. Sorry I'm a few minutes late." He slid the sunglasses up on his forehead. Surprise lifted them higher when his eyebrows shot clear up to his hairline. "Sophie?"

"Hi, Tanner." Her tone lacked any hint of joviality and when he smiled in greeting, she didn't reciprocate.

"Is this the someone's opinion you wanted?" Tanner turned to Cole, hand splayed in Sophie's direction.

"Well, I want more than just her opinion," Cole said, then realized his blunder, the potential for those words to be greatly misconstrued. "I mean, I want her opinion, yes, but mostly, her approval. Sophie's flower farm is on the same plot we'll be landscaping and it's vital that we incorporate it so it feels like one cohesive and intentional space."

"Never thought I'd be working on a project again with you, Soph. Can't say I'm disappointed one little bit."

Hearing Tanner call her Soph made his stomach tighten in discomfort. He hoped she hadn't experienced the same reaction each time Cole had used that nickname for her before.

"We weren't exactly working together on anything, Tanner," Sophie said in a manner so clipped, even Cole felt put in his place.

"Well, sure. Whatever you want to call it." He shrugged, then blurted, "Shoot, I left my contractor's card in the truck. Let me grab it real quick and catch up with you."

Cole and Sophie agreed to meet Tanner inside, so they turned to begin their walk up to Morning Glory Nursery. Cole's steps were just as hesitant as his voice when he inferred, "I take it you two have already met?"

Expelling a sigh, Sophie followed it with a groan. "We've met."

That didn't feel like the entire answer. "Listen, I'm not going to barrage you with a bunch of questions because it's really none of my business, so if you want to offer any more information, that's totally up to you. I just want to be sure that you're comfortable with Tanner managing things on the jobsite. He's going to be my point-man on this, but if he's any sort of threat to you, just say the word and I'll cut him loose."

"He's not a threat at all. Just a guy who couldn't take a hint."

"Gotcha." Cole rubbed at the back of his neck. "It's weird. I could have sworn he was right out of college. I didn't realize he was around your age."

"What makes you think *I'm* not right out of college?"

Cole's throat went dry. "Oh, I—"

"I'm teasing you, Cole. I graduated six years ago," she clarified. "And Tanner *is* right out of college, I think. He was actually just out of high school when we first met."

The large automatic doors yawned open, allowing Cole and Sophie to walk through. Air conditioning hit them with a chilled blast. Sophie turned to the right and pulled out a flatbed cart from the long line gathered along the wall.

"I didn't take you for a robbing-the-cradle sort of gal," Cole joked.

"I'm not. At *all*. He was the brother of one of my grooms."

"And just how many grooms have you had?"

"You know what I mean." Sophie jabbed the point of her elbow into his stomach and Cole wished he would've had more of a warning because he would've at least attempted to flex. "I did the flowers for his older brother's wedding several years ago and somehow, throughout the course of it all, Tanner came to the conclusion that we would make a great couple." She nodded toward the doors on the left side of the building that led to the outdoor patio where the potted plants were kept, indicating that was the direction they should head. Cole followed. "Must've been all those times I had to call him the *best* man that went to his head. All I know is that the day of the wedding, I'm pinning his boutonniere on his lapel and he goes in for a kiss. Completely shocking and not at all wanted, nor encouraged." Her shoulders lifted in a shrug. "I think he'd gotten ahold of some of the champagne intended for the toast and decided to start the festivities a little early. I figured after the big day it would all die down, but he called and texted for a solid month before I had to pretend to be dating someone else for him to finally get the hint."

"Well, if you need to pretend to be dating someone now to keep him off your back, I'm your man." This time Cole flexed, just in case another surprise jab was in store.

"I think I can handle him, but thank you."

At that moment, Tanner jogged up, his feet clapping loudly on the pavement like he was wearing flippers. "Found it." He flashed his store discount card. "So, Soph, how's life been treating you? It's been a while."

"Pretty good, Tanner. You?"

"Fantastic. I'm in between relationships, but you know, always looking."

"I'm sure you are," Sophie said through a tight-lipped smile.

Not that Cole wanted to encourage Tanner's behavior in any way, but he had to admit, seeing the two interact was enlightening. It was different from his own interactions with Sophie, even those when she had been trying her best to shut him out, back when she assumed Cole's only objective was to put her out of business. Underneath all of that disinterest, there was still an undeniable attraction that came across in her body language, her gaze, her speech. With Tanner, there wasn't any to be found.

The three strolled up and down the aisles for over an hour, and while Tanner clearly had no instincts when it came to women, the same couldn't be said for his horticulture knowledge. He was quickly able to identify the species of plants that would work best with their design plan, and it was a relief to Cole that Sophie was in agreement with the good majority of Tanner's suggestions. They each took notes, and at the end of their outing, they placed a large order with the store, planning to pick the shipment up after they'd broken ground at the site.

Tanner received a text from one of his employees at another job and hurriedly excused himself, which Cole couldn't say disappointed him at all. He walked Sophie to her car, but the fact that his own was parked immediately next to hers made the gesture feel considerably less chivalrous.

There they stood, that impending, awkward goodbye suspended between them. Throwing all caution to the wind, Cole took a step toward Sophie. He yanked her into his arms and pulled her tightly to his chest. The relief that flooded him when she snaked her arms around his waist, locking her hands at his back, made his pulse lurch into a racing tempo. He didn't want to let go. If he held her for just a few moments more, that innocent hug would turn into an embrace, and though everything *felt* right about prolonging the moment, he knew he had to take things slow if they were going to take things anywhere at all.

In all honesty, they would need to take things really

slow. Approximately two months slow. If Cole was going to win this contest for the McAllisters, a relationship with Sophie could only remain a far-off hope.

A far-off hope he could handle, so long as it didn't turn into a farfetched dream. He supposed only time would tell.

9

SOPHIE

"*W*HAT'S HIS FAVORITE food?" Sophie's mother, Geri, pulled a casserole out of the oven, scrunching her mouth in disapproval. "Well, that certainly still looks raw," she murmured to herself as she shoved the chicken enchilada dish back onto the rack and reset the egg timer on the counter for an additional ten minutes.

"I don't know his favorite foods, Mom. He's just a friend."

"But you haven't invited any friends over to our place for years now. I was beginning to think you didn't have any."

"Maybe Sophie doesn't bring anyone around here because she would actually like to keep the few friends she does have, Mom. Your cooking is enough to scare any potential suitor away." Sophie's brother, Derek, plunged a baby carrot into the dish of ranch dip and tossed it into his mouth. Sophie always made an effort to bring a vegetable platter to her parents for their Sunday suppers, if only to ensure that there would be at least one edible item on the menu for the night.

"He's just a friend, and that's even a stretch. More like a workplace acquaintance. We hardly even know each other, really."

"You don't see me inviting any of my workplace acquaintances to dinner now, do you?" Derek cocked his head, sizing up his sister in the judgmental manner only a sibling could get away with.

"And you think I would actually let you?" Caroline piped up from behind the bridal magazine she had cozied up with on the couch in the family room adjacent the kitchen. "It's bad enough that you share a desk with that bombshell Tammy Weathers every weekday morning from five to seven. We don't need to bring her around for dinnertime, too."

Derek padded across the room to plant a kiss on the crown of his fiancé's head. "Trust me, sweet Caroline, I don't want to spend more time with Tammy than my paycheck requires of me. People might not realize it, but news anchors often have to put on an act just as much as any movie star. That chemistry everyone mentions? It's utter fabrication. All about the ratings. I know you've seen Marcus and Maggie from Channel 7."

"The anchors that are always bickering and arguing like an old married couple?" Sophie could hardly stand to tune into their show. Their bristly on-air personality clashes were not the best way to start one's day. "It's physically uncomfortable to watch them."

"My point exactly." Derek strode back into the open concept kitchen and tossed carrot number two into his mouth like it was a piece of popcorn.

"Don't fill up on those," Geri scolded her son over his shoulder. She swatted his hand with a whip of a dishrag. "You're going to spoil your appetite."

Stretching across the counter toward Sophie, Derek whispered loudly enough for their mother to hear, "That's the whole plan."

Maybe Derek was right. If he could act like there was chemistry between he and his coworker, then surely Sophie would be able to act like there *wasn't* any chemistry with Cole. It couldn't be that difficult, especially considering she'd only known him less than a week.

Yet when the doorbell chimed his arrival, that slow growing confidence flew right out the window.

"Glasses is here!" Caroline blurted. She yanked the magazine up to her mouth and covered it, like she could shove the words back in with the help of the glossy pages. "That was really loud. Sorry!"

"Please don't call him Glasses to his face," Sophie begged. She wished Caroline hadn't slipped up like that. The fact that Cole had a nickname—albeit one Sophie hadn't actually assigned to him—was just further confirmation that he was more than the innocent coworker she'd made him out to be.

"Glasses?" Geri perked up. "Oooh! Does he wear glasses, Sophie? I've always loved a man in lenses."

"Mom!"

"I can't help it." Sophie's mother squeezed her hands together in front of her excitedly. "Like Clark Kent. *Superman*. Something so intriguing about a man with a good set of spectacles."

"This conversation is beginning to make me weirdly uncomfortable." Derek grimaced. "Just get the door, would you, sis?" He nudged a carrot toward the direction of the entryway.

"Yes! Don't keep the man waiting," Geri ordered.

Inviting Cole to their family dinner had been a terrible idea. Sophie wrote the evening off as a complete failure and Cole hadn't even set foot in the house yet.

Taking ahold of the knob, Sophie gathered a deep breath, steeling herself for the long, uncomfortable night ahead. She swung the door open wide.

"You all are crazy." There, standing on the porch, was her father, Jerry, a brown grocery sack in his hands and a disapproving frown tucked under his neat mustache. "Certifiably crazy."

"Dad, why are you using the front door?" Sophie scooped the bag from his hands. "And why did you ring the doorbell? Did Mom take your keys away again?"

Her father bent to sweep a kiss on his daughter's cheek as he crossed over the threshold and into the foyer. "I wanted to see what it would be like for a stranger to come into our home. It's been so long since we've had company other than you and your brothers, you know? Wanted a firsthand glimpse of what it felt like to be an outsider. We need some serious practice, Potters. This was not our best showing."

"We're not that bad," Geri attempted to negotiate with her husband.

"First of all, that's a solid, wood core door and you all are squawking so loudly I could hear every word of your conversation on the other side."

A guilty look shrouded Geri's features. "Every word?"

"I thought you gave up on your little Clark Kent fantasy years ago when I refused to wear spandex for that

Halloween party at the Markesan's," Jerry jabbed. He turned to the others. "Family, I would not say entertaining is our strong suit. If we're to impress this boyfriend of Sophie's, we need to up our game. Really polish our act. We're floundering at the present time."

"He's not my boyfriend!" Sophie shouted, the level of her tone rising with each word like someone had twisted the dial on her volume.

A throat cleared.

Sophie froze.

Mortified, she turned around, only to see Cole standing in the open frame of the door she had not yet closed. He had a plate of cookies in one hand, a potted succulent in the other, and he wore a broad, all knowing grin.

"Glasses!" Geri cooed.

Sophie shot her mother a warning glare, not that it would do anything. Her mother was in full-on swooning mode.

"Cole." Sophie stepped forward to take the dessert platter. "Come on in."

"You'll have to excuse my family. We don't get out much and sadly, we don't have visitors *in* much, either," Jerry explained as he placed a welcoming palm on Cole's shoulder and the other in his hand for a firm, fatherly shake. "It's a bit of a circus around here."

"I'm just grateful for the invitation, sir."

"Sir." Jerry spun around and made intentional eye contact with his son first, then his daughter. "Did you hear that, you two? *Sir.* How many years did I try to get you both to call me sir, and here's Cole, not even ten feet into our house and he's already got it down. I like him already."

"I believe you wanted us to call you Sir Potters, Dad." Derek explained. "We're not even a fraction British."

"Sir Potters. Just sir. Either works perfectly fine for me." Jerry waved his hand to welcome Cole further into the house. "Come on in, Cole, and make yourself at home. My name's Jerry and my wife is also Geri. We like to keep things simple around here."

"Short for Geraldine," Sophie's mom interjected through a ridiculous smile.

"Can I get you something to drink?" Jerry asked. "An old fashioned? Manhattan? A brewski?"

"I'm fine with water for now, thank you." If Cole noticed the painfully obvious awkwardness of the Potter family, he didn't let on. He took a step toward Geri and extended the small potted cactus. "This is for you, Mrs. Potters. I figured your house was probably full of flowers already, what with having a daughter who's a flower farming phenomenon and all."

"Phenomenon?" Derek spat. He nearly choked on a carrot. "Sophie? A phenomenon? Hardly."

"No," Cole said, "I actually read those very words in an online article about her flowers."

"Yeah, an article her *brother* wrote for a copy-editing class he was taking at the time."

"It's not my fault Scott thinks so highly of me, Derek. Maybe if you two could work things out, he'd actually have some nice words to say about you, too." Sophie knew it was a below-the-belt move, but she couldn't keep from flinging the words at her middle brother. Every time they were in the same room, they reverted back to their childish ways.

"That was harsh, Soph. Too harsh."

"You have another brother?" Cole asked. "There are even more of you?"

Like she had been hanging on his every word, Geri rushed over, her cell phone in hand, already swiping the screen. "There sure are more of us! I even have a new grandbaby, Cole! She's the most precious thing on this entire earth. I got to be there for her birth and everything. Right there in the delivery room, up close and personal. Look! I have a phone full of pictures!"

Smiling, Cole turned away from Sophie to study the images pulled up on Geri's phone. Sophie loved that her mother was such a doting grandmother, but she highly doubted Cole had any real interest in looking at the photos of a squished, wrinkly baby he didn't even know. Still, he didn't show it if it had been off-putting. He matched Geri's excitement note for note, even admiring the little details like Aimee's handmade flower headband and her onesie that read *I Love Grammy* across the front in pink glittering letters.

He was a good sport, plain and simple.

Realizing Cole could fend for himself, Sophie poured herself a glass of fresh-squeezed lemonade from the pitcher on the counter and decided to settle in with Caroline on the couch until the casserole was finished, which at the current rate, would be several hours, if at all.

"Should I do fondant flowers on the cake?" Caroline set her wedding magazine down on her lap and looked over at Sophie. "I love the look of fondant ones, but they are so time consuming to make and don't taste all that great. Since I've taken on the crazy task of making my own cake for this wedding, I think it might be wise to go with something else."

"You know," Sophie began, thinking out loud, "there are lots of varieties of edible flowers. Hibiscus and nasturtiums and bachelor's buttons. Let me ask around and see what I can get my hands on. Could be the ideal compromise and the perfect touch for your cake."

"Really, Soph?" Caroline's bright eyes widened excitedly. "That would be amazing!"

Just then, Sophie's phone buzzed in her pocket, alerting her to an incoming text. She pulled it up and frowned the moment she read the message on the screen.

"Bad news?" Caroline inferred from Sophie's expression.

"Kind of. Our musical talent just cancelled for the market on Tuesday. Apparently, the lead guitarist has shingles." Sophie sighed, daunted by the thought of finding a replacement on such short notice. "If it was any other market, it would be fine, but this is our first of the season. All of the fliers I posted throughout town advertised live music. Without that, it's going to feel so much less special."

Jerry walked over to the couch and dropped his hands onto his daughter's shoulders. "You know my offer still stands, sweetheart. Just say the word and I'll bust out the old six string."

"You play?" Cole joined the group gathered in the family room. He had some sort of pink fizzy drink in his hand which Sophie assumed her mother had concocted. Sophie laughed inwardly, realizing very little of the drink had been consumed, its color and consistency disconcerting.

"I dabble a bit," Jerry replied.

"That's an understatement. Dad used to be in a rock

band back in the day. What were you guys called again? The Peanut Butter Fish?"

"The Jam Fish—like a take on jellyfish, but with jam. Get it? Like a jamming session. And it was more of a duo than a band. We lost our drummer and bassist when they decided to get married and start a family right before we went on our west coast tour. That just left me and old Stumpy. We got a few gigs after that, but nothing noteworthy." Nostalgia filled Jerry's voice and his gaze. "Man, I wonder if I'd even be able to tune that old thing. I haven't picked up a guitar in years."

"Mind if I check it out?" Cole asked. He set his still-full glass onto the end table. "I'd be happy to see if I could help tune it. I play a little bit, too."

"Really? That would be aces!" Jerry smiled at Cole and winked at his daughter. "I like this one already, Soph. Keep him around as long as you like."

Sophie wasn't about to explain again that Cole wasn't her boyfriend. She'd already blurted that statement so loud she figured the neighbors had heard. Instead, she just smiled at her dad as he and Cole retreated to the den at the back of the house where Jerry kept his modest collection of musical instruments from his glory days.

"Well, isn't he a tall drink of water?" Geri plopped down onto the loveseat next to her daughter and soon-to-be daughter in law.

"And that's my cue," Derek blurted, following the same path down the hall to join up with the other men.

"Well, he is," Geri said again, unashamed. "Where on earth did you find him, dear?"

"He's doing a little landscaping for the McAllisters," Sophie answered.

"He's doing more than just a little landscaping for them," Caroline corrected. "They've entered the *Backyard and Beyond Summer Showcase* and Cole's their design architect. Not that I should even be saying any of this out loud."

"Why's that?" Geri asked.

"You haven't talked with Derek about this, have you?" Sophie hadn't had a chance to warn Caroline, and that lack of preparation had her feeling suddenly queasy. If Derek already knew who Cole was, then it was all over—all before it even had the chance to begin.

"Of course, I haven't," Caroline confirmed. "I'm no dummy, Soph. That reeks of conflict of interest."

Geri, who had poured herself the same drink she'd concocted for Cole, took ahold of it and drew it to her mouth for a sip. Her lips contorted into a look of disgust, realizing how truly awful it was. If only she had the same ability to self-assess her cooking, too. "Why's it a conflict of interest?"

"Because Derek's news station is sponsoring the showcase this year. No relatives of the station are allowed to be participants. It's the contest rules, like with radio stations and concert tickets and giveaways like that."

"But Sophie's not *designing* the backyard. She's not a contestant."

"The powers that be won't see it that way. If there's any sort of collaboration, she'll be considered one, too. Honestly, just her flower farm being on the same land might be enough to get them disqualified."

Geri hunkered down in the cushions. "So what's our plan? Keep Cole's true identity hidden? Create an alter ego?" She thought on it a moment, then her eyes grew wide. "Just like Superman and Clark Kent!"

"Cole's already registered as the landscape designer," Sophie explained. "We just have to make sure we keep our relationship under wraps."

"Relationship!" Geri hugged herself. "I never thought I'd hear you say those words! I knew there was hope for you yet, dear."

Sophie had misspoken, but still felt the insult. "Not that there *is* a relationship. I just mean, we can't be involved in any way."

"Too late for that," Caroline said. "I see the way he looks at you, Sophie. The man is smitten."

"Hardly."

"No, I'm serious. It's like there's no one else in the room." Caroline sputtered a laugh. "And that's hard to accomplish in a room filled with people as loud as the Potters."

"I'll give you that."

Just then, guitar strumming from the back of the house filtered into the family room, musical notes reverberating through the air. The familiar twang of Dad's guitar had Sophie instantly transported back to her childhood, back when her father would sing them to sleep, his guitar resting gently upon his knee while he sat on the hope chest at the foot of Sophie's bed. There was a deep comfort in the sound of that instrument and an even deeper comfort in her father's strong voice accompanying the melody.

But the voice that pulled up the fine hairs on the back of Sophie's neck didn't belong to her father. No, the rich, buttery tone was new—one she'd never heard before. There was a controlled power to it, an effortless range that spiked high and dove low, meeting each note with perfect pitch and tone.

Caroline's eyes went wide. "Is that—?"

"Cole?" Sophie breathed. "It must be."

"Oh, honey, you've got to snag that man! He's handsome *and* he can sing! I only lucked out with one of those particular traits with your father, and I'm not going to say which one."

Sophie almost couldn't register her mother's words, her attention fully seized by Cole's singing. Without meaning to, her eyes slipped shut, the timbre of his voice one of the purest sounds she'd ever heard. She got lost in it; swallowed up in the cadence and lilt.

"I think you've found your musical talent for Tuesday's market, Soph," Caroline said as she picked her magazine up and flipped back to the page where she had left off earlier. "And based on that smile on your face, I think you might've found even more than that."

10

COLE

"I'M SO SORRY you had to endure that, Cole." Sophie leaned against the bumper of Cole's rental car, her arms folded across her chest, hugging herself for warmth as she ran her hands up and down her biceps. There was a welcome chill to the air accompanying the delta breeze that had rolled in right after they finished dinner. It made for the perfect ambiance to sit on Sophie's parents' back deck with a mug of coffee in hand while Jerry recounted the rock band days of his youth. To Cole, it had been the perfect finish to a great evening spent in enjoyable conversation and company.

"I didn't endure anything," Cole answered. "Believe it or not, I actually had a good time with your family."

"You don't have to be nice just for the sake of being nice, Cole."

"I'm not." He held up his hand in a salute. "Scout's honor."

Sophie smiled, glancing up from under her dark lashes. The cresting moon reflected soft light across her face, highlighting the feminine angles and curves of her sloping cheekbones and parted lips. She held Cole's gaze when she said, "They really liked you."

"I really liked them."

I really like you, was actually on the tip of Cole's tongue, but he didn't let the words find their way out. He was unsure what to say next, but knew he didn't want their time together to end. He would prolong it any way he could. "Will you be at the flower farm tomorrow?"

"Yep, I plan to be."

"Me too. Want me to pick you up on my way?"

"I'd love that," Sophie said, smiling so brightly her eyes scrunched at the corners.

"Can I grab you a coffee?"

"That would be awesome. Decaf white mocha, please."

"Decaf?" Cole chuckled. "What's the point of even drinking coffee at all if it's going to be decaf?"

"I like coffee for its flavor, not necessarily for the caffeine."

"Said no one ever."

"Well then, that must make me the first."

"It must." He grinned from ear to ear. "Sophie." Cole paused, his eyes meeting hers as his brow lowered. "I really did have a great time tonight. I know you were just being nice by inviting me along, but I'm glad you did. I loved meeting your family, but if I'm being honest, I did notice your efforts to derail any conversation that had to do with the McAllister project. I just want you to know that if this contest is going to cause any problems within your family, then I'm out. I won't be the one to come between you and your brother. It's just another job for me."

"Cole, you and I both know that isn't true. This could be *the* job. The one to change everything for you."

"My career aspirations are far less important than your family's relationships, Sophie. I want you to know that."

"Things are good with me and my brothers. Maybe not great between the two of them individually, but I'm sort of the middleman in that way. Always have been. The peacemaker, you know?"

"Which is why I don't want to disrupt the peace."

"You're not, Cole. And this project won't, either. As long as we maintain a cordial, professional relationship, they can't really pin anything on us."

Cole stepped forward, lessening the space between them. "So we shouldn't be caught doing this?" In one fluid movement, he drew Sophie into himself, holding her tightly against his chest as he pulled her close with his hands placed at the small of her back.

Sophie melted. Her face met the warm crook of Cole's neck and she exhaled deeply, her breath feathering across his flushed skin. Cole rested his chin against the top of Sophie's head and allowed his eyelids to fall shut. He breathed in her intoxicating scent of lavender and vanilla, getting lost in the aroma. It had been so long since he felt this way about a woman. It startled him. They had met just days earlier, but the feelings he had for Sophie only intensified with each moment together. He almost didn't know what to do with them.

Drawing back, Cole placed a light kiss on Sophie's forehead.

"Cole—"

"I'm sorry, Sophie. I shouldn't have done that."

"No," she stuttered, eyelashes fluttering and her breath quaking out from her. "Please do."

Sophie placed a hand on either side of Cole's jaw and stood up on her toes to leave a soft kiss on his cheek. "I'll see you bright and early." She beamed. "With my *decaf* coffee."

∾

FOR NOT BEING able to be seen with one another, Cole and Sophie sure spent a lot of time together. All of Monday, they worked at the McAllister property, from the first break of sunrise to the waning moments of sundown. Sophie tended to her flowers while Cole met with Tanner and a few men from his team to further discuss the layout and design, and even though they didn't say more than a few words, the glances Cole and Sophie exchanged from across the yard contained a novel full of emotion. Cole's thoughts would wander while Tanner spoke about the permits he'd need to pull down at the county or the amount of lumber they would have to order. Cole physically had to shake his head to break from his reverie and tether himself back down to earth. He had the most ethereal feeling every time he thought back to the previous night with Sophie in his arms.

But he needed to focus.

Luckily, Kelly McAllister loved the proposed design and instructed Cole to get right to work on making it a backyard reality. There were a few items to adjust, but the overall concept was a go. Over the next few weeks, they had plans to build a set of miniature silos, an expansive patio pergola, a substantial working windmill, and redwood retaining walls to frame it all in. It would be his most intricate project to date and that excited Cole just as much as it intimidated him.

He spent the majority of Monday night working out the details of the project and stayed up much later than he should have rehearsing a few songs for the Farmers' Market the following evening. When Sophie had asked if he would be willing to play, Cole's kneejerk reaction was to say no. It had been years since he performed in any sort of public setting. But he would be lying if he said living in Nashville wasn't inspiration enough to pick his guitar back up. All one had to do was walk two blocks up Broadway. The talent was overflowing, spilling out of each bar and club. You could hear the hopes and dreams of tomorrow's Billboard artists echoing through every open door.

Cole was never one to aspire to any sort of fame, but he sure did love picking up a guitar and getting lost in song. That instrument became his companion right after Caleb had died. Back then, Cole had a hard time articulating his thoughts and feelings, especially when it came to his older brother's unexpected passing. He closed up. Shut down. But one of his brother's friends had gifted him a hand-me-down guitar for his sixteenth birthday and when Cole's fingers brushed the strings, it was like he had unlocked an entirely new language.

The emotions he couldn't put to words found notes instead. There was always a melody to match his mood, and that endless repertoire of emotion was a saving grace for Cole back in those lost, struggling years.

But as he prepared for his Farmers' Market debut, the only tunes Cole could summon from memory were the happiest, joy-filled ones. Maybe that was because those were the emotions he had experienced since setting foot in Fairvale. Cole practiced for hours, until his fingertips and voice were raw from overuse. But it felt so good to express himself this way again. Every melody had Sophie at the very heart of it. Her determined spirit echoed out in the staccato notes. Her soft, thoughtful glances were in the tender, quiet strums. And the jubilant, up-tempo rhythm was their growing relationship.

Sophie was as beautifully complex as a song, and that reality had Cole pulling out a sheet of blank paper to compose his own tune meant just for her. He couldn't keep from doing so.

～

WHEN TUESDAY ROLLED around, Cole knew Sophie would have her hands full as she prepared for the market. He had offered his help, but she'd declined, saying she didn't want to monopolize his time when she knew the McAllister project should be his number one priority. But somehow, over the course of just one short week, Cole's priorities had shifted.

Yes, he still wanted to win the contest, but that need to prove himself was no longer there. His ties back home and to the firm had loosened, and what mattered in the moment was Sophie. Her happiness. Her success. Cole wanted nothing but for Sophie to realize her dreams. That scared him, and if he was being honest, an admission of that sort would probably scare her, too.

So he decided to keep it to himself. Cole wasn't about to ruin things with premature declarations of affection. It was still so early on, anyway. Like Sophie's flowers, there were stages to a relationship. Flowers didn't start off in full bloom. No, they began as buds, bound tightly, protected from potential hurt or harm. Then, as though they slowly began to trust the outside world around them, they unfurled with gentle caution, each petal opening up more and more until they stretched fully, letting the sun wash over them in uninhibited splendor.

Getting to know someone—and falling for them—was a process not unlike the blooming of a flower. Cole and Sophie would need to take things slow if they were to take them anywhere at all.

But writing a song for her didn't feel like it fit into the "taking things slow" category. Cole figured she wouldn't even know it was about her. It could be about anyone, really. But the fact that he had composed it in under an hour, the words and the notes pouring out of him like a rushing stream of creativity, only made it even more clear that she had been his muse. A melody brought to life that quickly could only be achieved with someone meaningful as the inspiration.

~

COLE ARRIVED AT the market just as the vendors were popping up their tents. Farmers carried large cardboard boxes filled with ripe fruits and vegetables from their vehicles to be displayed on tables with red and white checkered cloths. There were sellers with lotions made from goat milk, and Cole even noticed a few florists selling wildflower-like bouquets wrapped in brown parchment and tied with twine.

There was a buzz about the community center parking

lot as it transformed from an asphalt oasis into a pop-up market filled with the county's best foods and wares. And there, in the very middle of it all was Sophie, clipboard in hand and a denim apron worn over a yellow sundress that twirled out at her slim waistline. She had on a floppy straw hat, the same one Cole had seen her wear in the garden, and her hair was swept into a low ponytail that trailed down her back.

She was breathtaking.

Cole hiked the strap to his guitar bag higher onto his shoulder and made his way through the crowd to reach her.

Sophie was in conversation with one of the vendors about tent placement, but when she caught Cole's gaze, she halted. An enormous grin burst onto her face.

"I will get that figured out for you in just a moment, Dante," she said with a reassuring hand placed on the man's forearm. "For now, you are welcome to set up next to Isabelle's Acres. I know Four Oaks Farm isn't going to be out here today, so there'll be an empty spot this week."

"That'll be just fine, Sophie," the man said. "Appreciate it."

"Let me know if you need anything else."

The man tipped his hat. "Sure thing."

Stepping forward, Sophie hurried over to Cole. "Hey! You made it."

"Of course I made it. I wouldn't miss this." Cole glanced around, taking it all in. "This really is fantastic, Sophie."

"This isn't even half of the vendors we have signed up for the season. It's still early. In a few weeks, we'll have even more flowers and produce. That's really when all of this comes alive." Her eyes lit up. "I've got you over by

Eagleton's Egg Farm. There's an amp and speakers already set up for you if you'd like to use them. I wasn't sure if you'd have them, considering you had to borrow Dad's guitar and all." She blew out a breath. "I'm sorry I asked you to do this, Cole, but you're really helping me out. I promise I'll find someone else for next week."

"I'm glad you asked me, Sophie. If you haven't noticed, making myself useful is one of my favorite pastimes. In fact, I was up all night practicing."

"Oh no! Really? I'm so sorry."

"Stop apologizing." Cole took Sophie's shoulders gently into his grip so they could lock eyes. "Please."

"Okay. I will. I tend to do that when I get frazzled. No more apologies."

"Good." Cole smiled and released her. "Can I help you with anything before I get started? Anything I can do to take the frazzled edge off?"

"Honestly? I think listening to your music will do just that. So go on, get set up and start serenading all of us with your seriously impressive singing skills."

11

SOPHIE

*S*OPHIE WAS DELIGHTED to see the turnout. For the first hour after the market opened, there was a steady flow of customers trickling through. By five-thirty, that trickle had turned into a rush. This was usually the case. Most shoppers would stop by the market after their long workday, sometimes to pick up items to prepare a meal back home, other times to make a meal of the fresh fruits and vegetables they sampled as they meandered from tent to tent.

Sophie loved seeing canvas tote bags bursting at the seams with market purchases. There was a comforting hum of conversation. It was like a hive of honey bees, that consistent white-noise buzz enveloping the entire space. As she walked the rows, Sophie noted the many smiles, handshakes, and hugs exchanged as shoppers reconnected with their favorite vendors. This was her favorite part of all. *Connection.* This was where their small town truly became a community.

"Soph!" Veronica Smithson peered over the heads of

several customers lingering at her booth, beckoning Sophie to her flower stand with a smile and wave. "Come check out the Queen Orange Lime zinnias! They're fabulous! You planted some this year, didn't you, doll?"

Sophie strode over to her friend's display. It was an attractive presentation of Mason jars with clusters of flowers and greenery. Sophie and Veronica had been friends for several years and often traded varietals when their own gardens lacked what they needed for a project or customer. They had even collaborated on a few weddings and baby showers in the past. It was a friendship grown from shared interests and talent and Sophie was so grateful for it.

"These are beautiful, Ver!" Sophie pulled the slender stalk from Veronica's hand and twirled it between her fingertips. The flower spun like a pinwheel. "Mine are just now beginning to bloom. Did you start these in your greenhouse?"

"You bet I did. First year doing so, actually. Truth be told, I think zinnias are plenty hardy and grow so well in our climate that I would've been just as successful direct seeding them again. Gotta admit, though, it sure is nice getting a few weeks' head start."

Sophie looked down at the flower and admired the intricate blend of colors into one thoughtful design, like watercolors spread on the petals. "I do envy you in that way. It's a dream of mine to have a greenhouse and get a jump on the season. But it's probably good that I don't have any flowers to sell yet. Starting up the market always seems to take all of my energy. Give me a few weeks, though. I'll be right out here with you. Up for a little friendly flower competition again this year?"

"Wouldn't have it any other way." Veronica turned to a customer in her line who wished to purchase a bouquet. "I'll catch up with you later, doll."

"Sounds like a plan."

Sophie spent the next hour checking in with each vendor, making sure they had their permits posted while she surveyed their inventory. She sampled so much delectable produce throughout her stroll, she nearly had a bellyache. Everything was mouthwatering and perfectly ripe, ready to eat.

By six-thirty, the market was in full swing. Cole's guitar provided a relaxing backdrop to the overall whir of the lot. Sophie could hear his full voice croon in and out over the noise, like a wave cresting and crashing the shores, then retreating back to sea. She couldn't quite make out the words to each song, but there were several beats she recognized from her dad's repertoire of go-to melodies. She assumed every musician had an inventory on hand, a selection of musical pieces they could pull from at a moment's notice.

Sophie walked the parking lot, enjoying the sights and sounds until she couldn't ignore the ache in her lower back, all of the stresses that led up to this night gathered there in her tense muscles. She knew it was time for a break, so she pulled up a folding chair beside Veronica and her table of flowers to rest a moment.

Sophie had purchased a raspberry lemonade from one of the new vendors and it provided much needed relief against the rising temperatures. It wasn't a particularly hot day, but the thermometer topped off in the mid-eighties, and with all her running around, that was warm enough for sweat to collect on Sophie's upper lip and gather in beads on her forehead. She pulled a handkerchief from her pocket and dabbed at her face with the cloth.

"Take a load off, Soph. Enjoy the sweet, sweet tunes," Veronica said, sashaying her hips back and forth to the classical guitar and splaying her arms out on either side like she was at a concert. "He's not too bad to look at, either."

Sophie's face heated. Grateful for the handkerchief, she hid behind it as she tried to mask her expression.

"Where on earth do you think he came from?"

Sophie shrugged, wordless.

"All I know is, I hope he stays around." Then, taking a cluster of flowers into her grip, Veronica turned to her friend. "Mind holding down the fort for me for a sec? I've got something I need to do."

"Sure thing," Sophie said, thankful for the out. Any longer and she would be spilling her guts not only about Cole's identity, but her growing feelings for him. That was information she definitely didn't need to share.

She didn't know what Veronica had up her sleeve, but figured it had to do with Cole based on the appreciative way she spoke about both his looks and talent. Following her with her gaze, Sophie watched Veronica thread her way through the market crowds and up to Cole, who was mid-song, his mouth only inches from the microphone. He acknowledged his visitor with a slight lift of his chin, but continued singing, not missing a single beat. When Veronica suddenly dropped down onto his lap, a flower held between her teeth like a tango dancer, Sophie's eyes almost tumbled out of her skull. Cole, being the good sport that he was, angled and adjusted his guitar slightly so he could continue to play, despite the woman literally throwing herself at him. Veronica snaked a hand around his neck and drew her mouth to his cheek, depositing a full, playful kiss along his square jaw. Then, just as suddenly as she appeared, she lifted off of his lap, turned her back in the most dramatic fashion, and tossed the remaining flowers over her shoulder. They landed in Cole's open guitar case at his feet.

"Just a little thank-you for sharing his talent." Veronica smirked at Sophie after she came back to the flower tent. "I think it took him a bit by surprise, but I doubt he can say he didn't enjoy it."

Sophie put her mouth on her straw and guzzled down the remaining contents of her cup. She had no real answer, nothing to say back to Veronica, but her stomach churned as she replayed the scene in her mind. Jealousy, green and all-consuming, coursed through her.

What did Sophie even have to be jealous about? Cole wasn't her boyfriend. And that was just a bunch of innocent flirtation. Veronica was like that, always had been. Her overconfidence was usually endearing and, often times, entertaining. Up until the moment she decided to sink her hooks into Cole. It alarmed Sophie that she would have such a strong, visceral reaction to seeing Cole with another woman, though.

Excusing herself, Sophie rose to throw away her empty lemonade cup. She wiped her hands on her denim apron and drew in a stabilizing breath. However shocking, she would not allow herself to become rattled by Veronica and her silly antics. No, Sophie would remain calm. Collected. Cool as the cucumbers for sale at Dante's tent.

She let herself get swept up in the joy of a rewarding first market of the season. From the looks of things, most vendors had a banner night, many selling out of their goods even before closing time. Some began packing away their tables and tents, shutting down for the evening, evidently satisfied with their successes, too.

It was dusk and the sky had only recently swapped out its bright blue hue for a more muted lavender. All in all, it was a gorgeous, fulfilling night. Sophie would choose to focus on those two things and not the stunt that Veronica had pulled. In truth, she doubted Veronica even gave it a second thought. She was a big flirt and that flirtation was not limited to Cole. Sophie knew that.

Choosing to end the evening on a high note, Sophie made her way through the dwindling crowds toward Cole. There really wasn't anywhere she could sit to take in his performance, so she walked the short distance to her truck in the adjacent lot and unlatched the tailgate. She hopped up onto it and let her legs dangle as though she were sitting on the edge of a pier, swinging them back and forth with the tempo. Cole hadn't noticed her, his eyes closed as he sang with all of his heart, his strong hands gripping the pick while he strummed. Along with the discarded flowers, Cole's guitar case held several crumpled dollar bills, meager tips from listeners that passed by. It was almost embarrassing, and Sophie realized she had no real business in asking him to perform at the Farmers' Market. He was a professional businessman, not a busker on the street. But the content look upon his face didn't hint at any sort of embarrassment. If anything, Cole seemed totally in his element, and when he started his final song of the evening, Sophie noticed that passion grow even more evident. His voice lifted with ease as he hit the highest notes, his range overwhelming and pure. But it wasn't Cole's effortless singing ability that made Sophie's throat ball into a tight knot. It wasn't even the melody.

It was the words.

> "She's spring and summer and I'm falling
> so hard for her.
> She's an unfurled flower with her beauty
> and grace,
> And everything seems to fall into place.
> When she's near, it's so clear, that I'm just a
> man with hopes as high as the sun,
> Praying she doesn't run
> Because if she does she'll take my heart
> And she sure feels like my perfect start."

She'd never heard it before, but that song somehow felt like a part of her. Like it beat right along with her very own heart, a pulsing rhythm spreading out into her body. This wasn't just a song. It was a love letter. A love letter Cole had clearly written for someone he held very special. Sophie wanted to be that someone more than she cared to admit and the thought of Cole singing it to anyone else made her hot with envy.

Maybe Cole wasn't even the original author of the song. That was the most likely scenario—that this was just another melody by some other artist and Cole just so happened to sing it that night at the market. Yet within the depths of her being—the same sacred space where she experienced that song so strongly—Sophie knew this wasn't the case. It couldn't be. Those lyrics came from the deepest part of Cole, too. And as she listened, she felt more connected to him than ever before.

She felt understood. She felt desired. She felt pursued, and though it seemed premature, Sophie couldn't keep the hope of something developing between them from unfolding within her heart.

She didn't want the song to end, but as with all songs, there was the anticipation of the final notes, the slowing in rhythm and the final decrescendo. Cole's voice gently trailed off and his hand fell away from the guitar. Turning his head, he caught Sophie's gaze. She offered a wave, but he just looked at her, his eyes brimming with emotion as his mouth lifted into a cautious smile, as though looking for some sign of approval.

Sophie's heart hammered in her chest, pounded in her ears. Cole settled his guitar in his case, right on top of the flowers and the dollar bills, and rose to his feet. Making measured strides across the gravel toward Sophie, Cole never broke eye contact.

Sophie didn't know what to say, her words failing in the moment as much as her composure.

Then, in an instant, his hands were on her shoulders and his lips were on her forehead, warm, full, and soft.

A sigh escaped Sophie's mouth. Sliding forward on the tailgate, she leaned in toward Cole, wrapping her arms around his firm, muscled back, drawing him close to her body and holding him with all she had.

"Do you feel this between us?" he asked in a hushed, tender voice. "Please tell me you feel it."

"I feel it."

He drew back. "I know we're not supposed to be anything. My brain knows that. It does. But you'll have to tell that to my heart. It hasn't quite figured it out."

"I think maybe it *has* figured it all out, Cole. I know mine has."

Sophie had wanted to ask if that song was for her, but she didn't need to anymore. In that moment, her heart told her all she needed to know.

12

COLE

*H*E HAD BEEN too bold. He knew that, but he didn't regret it. If anything, Cole wished he would have been even more forward. Upfront and honest about the song he'd written just for her. He wanted Sophie to know she had been his muse, his reason for putting a pen to paper. He wished he had told her so.

But something in her smile and in the vulnerable tone of her voice told him he didn't need to explain anything. She already knew.

The next few weeks passed more quickly than Cole wanted them to. Usually, he liked when a project would sail by, gaining speed as things fell into place, that snowball of successes and achievements. The end result was always his motivating factor. Cole wasn't in the race to look at the scenery as he ran toward the finish line. Yet this time around, he found himself distracted by his surroundings at every turn, like he couldn't keep his eyes fixed on the prize.

In fact, he had to keep reminding himself exactly what that prize was. Last month, he would have said it was the *Backyard and Beyond Summer Showcase.* Obviously. But if someone were to pose that question to him now, his answer would be vastly different. Sophie's heart was the prize. That was all he wanted and if the entire backyard competition went away and she stayed, that would be just fine with Cole.

There were times he contemplated bowing out of the design contest altogether. Cole could leave it in Tanner's capable hands, confident it would turn out just fine. Better than fine, even. But it was Sophie's relationship to her brother that threw a monkey wrench into things. The only way to make everything aboveboard would be if Sophie didn't farm the very land involved in the competition. It wasn't even an option to think along those lines.

Instead, they became quite good at hiding their growing feelings, in public at least. Cole refrained from singing any love songs directed toward Sophie at the markets, and when the two happened to be at the McAllister's at the same time—which was almost daily—they rarely so much as made eye contact. Cole trained his gaze not to follow Sophie as she strolled the rows, her flowers now stretching up to her waist like she was dressed in their splendor. It took great effort and determination, but Cole managed.

The hardest part was not being able to take Sophie out on a date. He wanted so badly to go back to Aromatizzare again. The mouthwatering Lover's Special taunted him. But Sophie was adamant they couldn't be seen with one another, especially sharing a meal in a romantic setting.

Sometimes they would eat in, at Cole's rental home mostly, so as to avoid Caroline and Derek and any questions their togetherness might bring about.

Because of the necessary secrecy, Cole often found himself wondering if Sophie shared his feelings. They were close in a more-than-friends sort of way, but other than a goodnight hug, they had little-to-no physical interaction. Cole was okay with that. He liked to take things slow. Even still, he couldn't help but wonder what her warm hand would feel like in his. Would their fingers thread perfectly together? He already knew he loved the way she fit right against him when he held her, how her head met his collarbone like it was meant to rest there.

Sure, he liked all of these physical things about Sophie, but more than that, Cole had grown to deeply admire her. It was no secret she was well respected in the community. It seemed as though everyone was a friend of Sophie's and had a story to share about a time when she'd saved their day in one way or another. It was amazing how flowers could do that: create meaningful memories for those on the receiving end of a bouquet.

But Cole gathered it was more than just the flowers that people thought back on so fondly. Without a doubt, it was Sophie behind them. She was like Midas with her golden touch, turning everything in her field into its most breathtaking version of itself. Sometimes, when Cole would run to the supermarket to pick up a few items, he would stroll through the floral department with his cart, just to take a peek at the arrangements they sold there. While the simple beauty of a flower couldn't be contested, there was something missing, something to take the bouquets to the next level. That something was Sophie.

Today Cole would have the honor of watching Sophie take her work to that next level firsthand. To his surprise, she'd invited him to accompany her to a client's wedding. Not as a date, Cole knew that, but still, the thought of seeing Sophie totally in her element intrigued him. With each market, his feelings for her grew stronger. He could only imagine what a wedding would do to increase that emotion. It almost scared him.

He rose early, unsure what to wear for a wedding. He hadn't brought much out from Nashville, but he did have a few options to sort through. Pulling three slacks from the closet, he paired them with matching button-up dress shirts and stood back. To Cole, they all looked the same.

He needed a woman's discerning opinion.

Reaching for his phone on the nightstand, Cole pulled up the number. On the second ring, she picked up, her face illuminating the screen.

"Hey. I need your advice."

"Good morning to you, too," Trista said, groggily. She thrust a fist into her eye and rubbed hard.

"Isn't it almost ten o'clock there?"

"Yes, Cole, it is. But it's a Saturday. The only day of the week that I don't have to spend my morning tying shoelaces and wiping snotty noses."

Trista was a preschool teacher, and while Cole knew she adored her job and her students, he could sense her frustration. He'd woken her on her day off. Sunday mornings she volunteered in the children's ministry at their church, which left Saturday as her only day of rest.

"I'm sorry, sis. I'll call back later."

"No. It's fine. I'm up now. You said you needed advice. What about?"

"Clothes."

A laugh pierced through the phone. "Okay, what's her name?"

"What do you mean? I just need help picking an outfit."

"Cole, you and I both know the whole twin intuition thing is real, but I don't even need that to know this is about a girl. In our thirty years, you've never asked me for advice about what to wear. Not even for your senior pictures, which was unfortunate because you really should've asked for my input then. That striped hoodie was atrocious."

"It was in style at the time."

"It was terrible. And the worst part is, Mom still has your photo framed on the mantle. I have to see it every time I go over there, Cole. You in all of your zebra sweat-shirt unsightliness. I'm going to steal that picture one of these days and burn it."

Looking down at the selection sprawled out on the bed, Cole noticed the black and white pinstriped shirt he had paired with dark slacks. They did have the potential to look zebra-ish. Immediately, he gathered the shirt, crumpled it into a ball, and tossed it across the room near the hamper. He flipped the camera around on the phone.

"Which of these do you like best?"

"What's it for?"

"A wedding."

Trista clucked. "You got invited to a wedding already? Haven't you been there less than a month?"

"I wasn't really invited."

"So you're crashing it?"

"No, I'm not crashing it, Trista. I'm just tagging along with a friend."

"But you weren't invited. This is really confusing."

Cole groaned. "The florist asked me to come along to help."

"And I take it this florist is female?"

"Not that it matters, but yes."

"And you like her."

"Trista, will you just help me pick an outfit?"

"I need to know if you like her, so I can make my decision based on that info."

"She's a friend."

"Oh, please, Cole. This is your twin you're talking to. I know you're lying even when you don't know you're lying."

Cole sighed, relenting. "Okay, I might like her a little bit."

"So you want to look your best?"

"Yes. That would be ideal."

"In that case, you should start with a haircut. You know I hate it when it starts curling over your ears and the arms of your glasses. You look like a shaggy sheepdog."

"I don't have time for a haircut. I'll just brush it."

"Brushing your hair is a given, Cole. Have you *not* been brushing your hair?" Bringing her hand up to her face, Trista smacked her forehead in exasperation. "Please tell me you are tending to your basic hygiene needs, Cole. What has California done to you?"

"I've been brushing my hair."

"And your teeth?"

"Yes, I've been brushing my teeth. Will you please just help me pick out some pants and a shirt?" He flipped the camera around on the phone and narrowed his eyes. "Do *any* of those work?"

"Turn me back around. I didn't really look."

"Because you were too busy harping on me about my hygiene."

"Good hair and breath are important when trying to woo a woman, Cole."

"I'm not trying to woo her."

"Then what exactly are you trying to do?"

He thought on it. "Okay, maybe I am trying to woo her."

"I knew it. You're in love!"

"I am definitely not in love. I've hardly known her a month."

"Doesn't matter. I've fallen in love in shorter time. When you know, you know. Unfortunately, none of those whirlwind relationships lasted, but man, were they incredible while they did." A wistful gleam came to Trista's eye as she reminisced. "I wonder what ever happened to Carlos. Gosh, he was handsome."

"All I know is that I really care about this woman. More than anyone I've cared about in a long, long time. I don't want to show up at the wedding venue and embarrass her—"

"By looking like a shaggy sheepdog."

"Sure, whatever. By looking like a shaggy sheepdog. Just tell me what to wear, Trista. Please?"

"I'd go with the gray pants and the navy and white checkered shirt. Not too formal, not too casual. And roll the sleeves up to your elbows. Women like forearms and you have nice, toned ones."

"That's weird."

"Trust me." Trista yawned. "If that's it for now, I'm going back to bed. If you need me, don't call until it's at least noon, east coast time."

"I think I can take it from here," Cole said. "Thanks, sis. Love you."

"Love you, too."

~

COLE FOLLOWED HIS sister's advice and wore the gingham shirt, even though he felt like a picnic tablecloth. He would just have to trust her judgment on this one.

At 8:30, he left his rental home to head over to the wedding venue, stopping by Heirloom Coffee to grab two drinks on the way: an Americano for himself and a decaf hibiscus latte for Sophie. When he pulled up to the big, red barn just fifteen minutes outside of town, he could see that Sophie had already been hard at work. Even the sign instructing guests where to park was adorned with her flowers. It was a delicate contrast to the gravel road and wooden fencing that welcomed wedding invitees onto the property. Cole parked, rolled up his sleeves as Trista had instructed, and stepped out of the car, coffee drinks in hand.

The property was abuzz with commotion, like the frenzied action of a movie set. Inside the barn, caterers lined up metal buffet trays with unlit warmers underneath. Others spread round tablecloths over bare tables, smoothing the wrinkles before settling napkins and utensils onto the surface. There were stacks of folding chairs being unloaded from vans parked just outside. Everyone was in their designated position with a specific job to do—

all cogs in a productive wheel—including Sophie, who stretched up on her tiptoes to fiddle with a sprig of greenery in a centerpiece.

"Brought you a little something." Cole handed her the cup, leaning in for a hug. He stopped short when he noticed the woman from the Farmers' Market behind her. Even though it had been weeks, he recalled her bold introduction on opening night quite clearly.

"Cole, you remember Veronica." Sophie took the drink and lifted it to her mouth, taking a long swallow. "Thanks for this." She smiled. "Just what I was craving."

"You're welcome. And yes, of course, I remember."

"How could you forget, right?" Veronica interjected. She elbowed him. "I've been told I make quite an impression."

"You got this, Ver?" Sophie turned to her friend. "I'm going to take Cole to the altar and have him help me set up the arbor. Other than delivering the bouquets and boutonnieres, that's the last thing on our to-do list."

"*Take Cole to the altar*," Veronica snickered under her breath. Sophie's cheeks noticeably flushed. "Sure, doll. I've got this covered. I'll get the rest of the centerpieces in place and then head out. Great work today, as always."

Leading the way through the open barn doors, Sophie stepped into the summer sun, the light washing over her in warm, brilliant rays. Deep auburn strands glistened in the hair that tumbled down her back in loose curls.

Cole stared unabashedly.

"What?" Sophie asked. "What's wrong?"

"Nothing's wrong, Sophie," Cole replied. "Everything's perfect."

She smiled, then took him by the elbow. "Okay. I've

got the boughs in the back of the truck. Let's go grab them and get them hung and then we'll head back to my house to get the rest of the flowers for the wedding party."

They made quick work of decorating the arbor. Even without Sophie's flowers, it was eye catching with its white birch branches standing tall and formed into a rustic arch. But when she adhered her eucalyptus boughs to the top corners with dozens of pale peach and mint flowers tucked into the leaves, it became a true work of art.

Sophie stepped back, thumbing her chin. "That cluster of peonics feels too heavy up at the top there. Can you help me spread them out? I think if we move a few to the other corner, it will look more balanced."

"Of course; happy to help. But you'll have to tell me which ones they are."

"You know, for a landscape architect, I would've thought you'd have a bit more knowledge when it comes to flower varietals."

"I've never really considered myself a big flower guy, I guess." Cole shrugged his shoulders. "Give me a shrub or a tree and I can probably name it, but flowers all seem kind of the same to me. Just colorful things with petals. Except for roses, I suppose. Those thorns really set them apart."

"I think every flower has something that sets it apart." Sophie said. "And it's not just the way a flower looks. It's been said that peonies symbolize a happy life and a happy marriage. I think that makes them so fitting to adorn an altar, don't you?"

Cole looked down at Sophie in awe. He loved the way she viewed things and how much of herself she put into her work. "I think it makes them the *perfect* flower. What other flowers have meanings?"

"Oh gosh. Nearly, all of them. Some mean what you think they would mean, like roses symbolizing desire and love. But then there are others like daisies and innocence. Or lavender, which is said to represent devotion and virtue. But my favorite is the yellow carnation."

"What does that one mean?"

Sophie snickered. "Rejection."

"Seriously? So you mean if you give someone a bouquet of yellow carnations, you're essentially rejecting them? With flowers?"

"Well, yeah. In sort of a passive-aggressive way, I suppose." Her lips curled up deviously. "Not that *I've* ever done anything like that."

Cole sensed her sarcasm immediately. "Why do I have a feeling even your break-ups involve flowers in one way or another?"

"It was only after the guy had flowers delivered to my house everyday for a week. I told him I wasn't interested in dating anyone at the time—that I had too much on my plate—but he didn't take the hint," she elaborated. "So I sent him a bouquet of my own with a note attached that said, *'Thank you for all of the flowers, but I feel the yellow carnation best symbolizes where our relationship is ultimately headed.'* After that the flowers stopped coming."

"Ouch!" Cole chuckled. "I'm beginning to see this as a constant thread throughout all of your relationships."

"What's that?"

"That the guy can't take a hint. Tanner. The poor daily flower delivery dude. I'm beginning to wonder if I'm in that same boat and just don't know it yet."

"You are definitely not in that boat, Cole. If I were to give you a bunch of flowers, they would be all gardenias. Every single one."

"And just what do gardenias mean?"

Sophie smirked, then said, "It's a secret."

SOPHIE

*S*OPHIE DOUBTED COLE picked up on the double meaning in her words, but that was okay. It was sort of fun to watch his brain turn as he tried to decipher her intention.

Secret love.

That's exactly what their relationship had become. Of all the flowers, the gardenia was the perfect expression of that. The last month with Cole had been a beautiful one, but the privacy behind their growing relationship forced everything into a corner of Sophie's life that she couldn't share with anyone else. On the nights she would come home from Cole's house after having dinner together, she would need to formulate a story to feed to Caroline and Derek regarding her whereabouts. That's what she hated the most: the inherent dishonesty in the secrecy.

Sophie had suddenly taken up hot yoga, wheel thrown pottery at the YMCA, and researching her Irish ancestry down at the local library. All of which were untrue, of course, but she had to form believable reasons for why she had plans nearly every evening. Caroline was a smart woman. Sophie knew she didn't buy any of it. But it wasn't Caroline she worried about. It was her brother.

Up until that point, Derek hadn't even mentioned Cole's name. Not even Glasses.

She had a feeling all of that was about to change.

~

"SOPHIE, EVERYTHING TURNED out better than I could have ever imagined!" Marie grabbed Sophie's arms and squeezed, drawing her into a huge hug, her billowing white gown bunched between them. "I couldn't've asked for a more perfect florist. It's all just so beautiful." Marie's bottom lip started to quiver.

"No you don't," Sophie said, tapping the bride on her chin. "Don't you dare mess up that beautiful wedding day makeup."

"I'm sorry," she sniffed. "It's just so overwhelming, you know? This day has been a dream of mine since I was a little girl. I just never thought it could be *this* magical. I know you're a big reason it is."

Just then, Peter came up to his new bride, two glasses of bubbling champagne in his hands. He wore the proudest grin. "Mrs. Niles, we're being requested back at the head table. Sounds like the toasts are about to begin."

"I'll catch up with you later," Sophie said. "Go enjoy your big day."

"Thank you again, Sophie. You're truly the best. I mean that."

Sophie's heart squeezed as she watched the newlyweds thread through the tables toward the wall of the barn where the rest of their wedding party had already taken their seats. The way Peter placed his hand low on his wife's back to guide her made something unfurl deep within Sophie's stomach. *Longing*. She hadn't known it, but oh, how she wanted that in her life. A partner. Someone to walk with and guide her. She swept her finger near the corner of her eye to catch an unbidden tear from escaping.

"That potato bar is out of this world. You've got to try it, Soph."

Turning around, Sophie saw Cole walking up to her, a bowl with tendrils of rising steam in his hand.

"They've got all the usual toppings like bacon bits and cheese and sour cream, but I suggest you go with the less traditional smoked salmon and grilled corn. Add the Sriracha and you've got a serious party in your mouth." He froze as he brought his fork to his lips. "Hey, are you alright?"

Sophie sniffed and rolled her shoulders. "Yes. I'm fine."

"You sure? You know, I've heard it's pretty normal to cry at weddings. At least that's what Trista always says when there's a wedding scene in a romantic comedy. She never watches those silly movies without a box of tissues handy."

"I'm not crying." Sophie swiped at her eyes again with the back of her hand, surprised when it came back wet. "Okay, maybe I am a little. I'm not really sure what's gotten into me. I've been to more weddings than I can count. Usually I can keep it together better than this."

Cole set his half-eaten potato down on the ledge of a nearby table. "You don't have to keep anything together, Sophie. If I'm being honest, I got a little choked up during the vows, too. All of that *to have and to hold* stuff. Kind of makes you reflect on your own life, I guess."

"Do you think about getting married?" She couldn't keep the words from tumbling out and hoped Cole didn't think she meant getting married to her. That would be entirely too presumptuous, even though he'd once teased Sophie that she was exactly that.

"Do I think about getting married? All the time. This?" He glanced around the barn, at the hundred or more friends and family that came out to celebrate Marie and Peter's special day. "I'd love to have this someday. A big, public declaration of love and commitment. I always just figured it would happen for me, but then life sort of got in the way."

"I get that. Mine did, too."

Sophie suddenly felt Cole's warm fingertips brush against her skin. Before she could react, his large hand covered hers, his fingers weaving with her own.

They stood there, in the back of the barn, off to the side and nearly out of sight, holding hands throughout the duration of the toasts. When the best man shared a story that garnered a laugh from the crowd, Cole's hand squeezed just so slightly. And when the maid of honor spoke of one day finding her own true love, Sophie couldn't help but zero in on Cole's thumb that swept back and forth softly over her skin.

She felt herself release the breath she'd kept trapped for the last month.

Despite the commotion around them—the hoots and hollers from guests as they clinked their forks to their glasses, requesting the bride and groom to share a kiss—it felt like Sophie and Cole were the only people in the entire space. Sophie could sense a tingle in her fingertips, could feel her pulse thrumming strongly in her wrist, all of her attention zeroed in on just that small portion of her body.

"Lovely reception, isn't it?"

Sophie yanked her hand from Cole's grip and spun around.

"I'm sorry, I don't believe we've formally met." Tammy Weathers slipped a manicured hand out to Sophie, her unnaturally plump lips forming an intimidating smile. "You might have seen me on T.V. I'm Tammy—one of the Channel 12 News anchors."

Cole snorted, then attempted to disguise it as a cough.

"Hi Tammy," Sophie said politely. She took the woman's hand into her own. "I'm Sophie. And we have met. Several times. My brother shares a desk with you every weekday morning."

"You're a Potters? I had no idea. I just came over to compliment you on the flowers. You've done a lovely job with them. Just lovely." Tammy batted her false lashes. "Wow. Small world, isn't it?"

"Indeed it is," Sophie replied, tightlipped.

Then, turning to Cole, Tammy's eyes narrowed. "You, I do know." She waggled a finger his direction as though trying to place him. "The backyard design contest! You're one of the architects, aren't you?"

"I am. I'm landscaping the McAllister project." Cole's tone was flat and impassive.

"Right, right. I'd recognize that face anywhere. How are things going? If I'm not mistaken, we should have a crew coming out to the property early next week to film."

"Things are going great," Cole said. "Everything's coming along nicely."

"Glad to hear it." Swiveling back to Sophie, Tammy asked, "And I heard you grew almost all of these flowers at your farm, Sophie. That's a pretty incredible feat."

"I did."

"Isn't that something? You know, I'd love to talk with my network to see if they'd be interested in doing an interview out at your flower farm. I'm working on a new segment called *Finding Fairvale* where we hope to interview and showcase local talent. I think you'd be perfect for it. Is that something you'd be up for?"

Sophie's throat tightened, making a swallow difficult. "Um, I suppose—"

"Do you happen to have a business card I could take with me?"

Eyes wide, Sophie sucked in a breath. If she gave Tammy a card, she would see right away that her farm was owned by the McAllisters, the address on it betraying her.

"It's no problem if you don't have one. I can easily get your information from Derek." Tammy popped open her clamshell purse and retrieved a small paper, slipping it between two fingers before flicking it toward Sophie. "Here's mine. Give me a call if it's something you're interested in. Could be really great for business." She turned to Cole. "And I'll see *you* next week. Can't wait to see this project firsthand."

Once out of earshot, Sophie sputtered a breath. "What am I going to do?"

"Just tell her you're not interested. Seemed like it was just a casual ask."

"No, Cole. What am I going to do when the news crew comes out this week to film your project? It's not like I can hide two acres of flowers."

"If they give us advance notice, we can just make sure you're not there. Or I can take credit for your garden. If you like, I'll even paint my thumb green so it's more convincing."

Sophie knew Cole was joking and only meant to assuage her fears, but his comments did little of the sort. Instead, she felt panic bubbling up within her, that awful feeling of getting caught in a lie that seemed to offer no escape.

"This isn't going to work," she suddenly blurted, then raced toward the barn doors.

The evening air rushed over her skin, pulling goose bumps up along her flesh. The breeze was biting enough that it caused her to shiver deep in her bones and wish she'd brought her sweater with her. With determined strides, she quickly crossed over the grassy knoll at the front of the wedding venue and made her way toward the parking lot. When she reached her truck, she yanked on the door handle and all but fell into the cab, defeat washing over her in unrelenting waves.

Sophie gathered her sweater from the seat and balled it up. She lifted it to her face and a frustrated gargle ripped from her throat, muffled into the soft fabric.

"You okay?"

Sophie jumped so high in her seat, she almost hit her head on the inside roof.

She threw her sweater at the intruder. "Cole! You scared me to death! I didn't hear you open the door."

"Because you were too busy yelling into your shirt." He handed her back the offending cardigan and cautiously climbed into the truck. "Sophie, did I say or do something back there to make you run?"

"You? Gosh, no, Cole. I'm just—it's just..." Her words trailed off as her gaze shifted to her hands in her lap. "I don't know. Things were so much easier before this whole backyard competition, you know? I had my flowers and the market and none of it was a threat to anyone."

"Your flowers aren't a threat, Sophie. In fact, other than those deceptive yellow carnations, flowers are the exact opposite of threatening."

She ran a hand through her hair, aggravated that he didn't understand. "I appreciate the levity, Cole, I do, but I'm being serious. It never occurred to me that something I love doing would ever pose a problem for someone else."

"I'm failing to see the actual problem." Cole looked at Sophie intently, searching out her eyes. "I think we've been doing a pretty good job keeping everything balanced and above reproach. It hasn't been easy, I know that, but I think it's been worth it."

"We have done a decent job, but it's exhausting."

Slumping against the seat, Cole blew out a breath. "I don't want to exhaust you, Sophie. That's never what I intended."

"That's not at all what I'm saying. You're not getting it." Sophie shook her head back and forth.

"Then tell me what you mean because all I'm hearing is that this landscape project is ruining your flower farm and that this—," he waved his hand frantically between them, "what we have developing here—is exhausting to you. Honestly, the only way I can see to fix it is for me to go back to Nashville and for your world to go back to the way it was before I ever came into it." He shrugged and Sophie noticed the tense muscle pulse in his jaw. Cole was rigid, teeth clenched, as he stared straight through the windshield. "I'd do that in an instant, Sophie, if you thought it would solve things. I would. But I hate to break it to you—it would only be a temporary fix to your problems at the farm."

"What do you mean by that?"

"The McAllisters said they weren't planning to renew your lease after this year."

Sophie's throat went dry, that awful parched sensation she couldn't control. "When did they tell you that?"

"The first day I met Kelly out at the property."

Sophie's eyes fell wide open in shock. "You've known for a month that this would be my last season on the farm and you never bothered to tell me?"

"It's not like I was trying to keep it from you, Sophie. It was sort of mentioned in passing. I honestly just didn't think about it much after she first told me."

"Well, then. I suppose that right there is the real problem."

"What is this problem that you keep referring to?"

"The problem is that my future isn't a part of your future, Cole. That the reality of me not having a place to farm next year didn't seem to impact you at all—to the point that you didn't even give it a second thought, or feel like you should at least give me a heads up." Her words were choppy with trembling breath. "That you would just flit into Fairvale, win your silly little contest, and then be merrily on your way. That *I'm* not a part of your future, Cole."

Cole's jaw ticked. "I didn't realize you thought what I do is silly."

"That's not what I meant," Sophie backpedaled.

"I think I should probably go."

"Cole—"

He turned in his seat. "Listen, I'm not upset with you. I'm not. I just think maybe we should put some space between us right now. I don't like where things are heading with this conversation and I don't want either of us to say something we'll regret."

"I think that might have already happened."

Sophie was used to big displays of emotion, but their conversation spun her completely around, leaving her disoriented and dizzied. She felt like screaming, she felt like crying, but mostly, she felt like being alone.

Cole picked up on that.

He reached for the door handle. "Drive safely and get some sleep, Sophie. It's been a big day."

"It has."

"We'll catch up later, okay?"

"Okay," was all she said as Cole stepped out of the vehicle, the cheers, laughter, and celebratory music pumping from the barn at odds with everything she felt in the pit of her stomach and in her aching heart.

COLE

"YOU HAVE THE perfect face for the camera, Cole." Tammy reached out and smoothed a piece of Cole's hair that fell across his forehead and then adjusted his glasses so they sat squarely upon his nose. It was like she was primping a child on school picture day. "I'm surprised you don't get approached all the time by talent scouts in Nashville. Rumor has it you sing, too. You're a triple threat: looks, smarts, and a set of pipes."

"Singing is just a hobby of mine," Cole admitted. A hobby he hadn't practiced in the last week, his standing invitation to perform at the market evidently withdrawn. He didn't expect Sophie to ask him back, not after the way they left things at Marie and Peter's wedding, but he still felt that disappointment in knowing she obviously didn't want him at the market.

"Well, I know I'm not supposed to have favorites, but this project is at the top of my list. It's all so impressive, Cole. You're quite good at what you do and it shows."

"Sorry I'm late!" Just then, Derek jogged up to Tammy, Cole, and the cameraman, huffing with labored breath. He bent over at the waist to collect himself with his hands pressed to his knees like he had just completed a 5K race. "I didn't realize we were doing this today. Just finished up at the gym. Gotta do something to get this body in wedding day shape!"

"Didn't you accept my calendar invite for this?" Tammy's mouth squiggled into a frown.

"I did, but with the wedding this Saturday, my brain's been elsewhere. Caroline's had me tasting cake flavors every night this week," Derek said. "Which reminds me, I need to go back in and get refitted for my tux this afternoon. I have a feeling my pant size has been paying the price for all these samples." He patted his stomach with a flat palm. "Anyway, I'm here now, so let's get started."

Tammy handed Derek a folder. "I've already prepped Cole with the interview questions, and we've done our portion with Kelly back at the house. It shouldn't take more than an hour to run through everything."

"That's good news," Derek replied. "Caroline's got me picking up the programs at noon and then I'm supposed to meet the caterer to drop off the final check. After that, I've got to circle up with the DJ about song choices. Caroline has a whole list of last minute changes. Seriously, my head is spinning so hard, it feels like it's going to fall right off."

"I'm happy to help if you need any," Cole suggested. He didn't know Derek well, but it was clear the man was being pulled in a thousand different directions. With the landscape project nearing completion, Cole found more free hours in his day than normal, and it would be good to fill them with something to keep his mind off of Sophie and their last conversation.

"Normally I would say I've got it all under control, but that couldn't be further from the truth. I just might take you up on that offer, Cole. Thanks, again. Just don't let anyone know how we know each other," Derek said with a wink.

"Not a problem at all. Happy to help."

Arms folded across her body, Tammy tapped an impatient foot on the newly installed brick walkway. "Well, *we* will certainly have a problem if we don't get the footage we need for this segment. If you're all done talking wedding woes, I suggest we get started."

∼

EVEN THOUGH TAMMY said he was a natural on camera, Cole felt anything but. His words were jumbled, his eye contact all wrong, and he misspoke more than once about the shrubs they had used for the hedges. He was grateful when Tanner showed up with a few guys from the crew, as it took a bit of the pressure off, and he was in need of a break from the scrutinizing camera lens.

"You're doing just great." Derek walked over to Cole and handed him a bottle of water before he sat next to him in a white Adirondack chair. "Tammy can be a bit intense, but she knows what she's doing and she's good at it. Your project photographs really well and you've done an awesome job explaining the process. I think the McAllisters are a big contender for the winning title this year, but don't tell anyone I said that."

"That's the goal, I suppose." Cole took a refreshing

swig of water, swishing it in his mouth. "It doesn't sound like it's an option to lose."

"Do they have plans to sell?"

"Not that I know of. Why?"

"I only ask because last year's winners put their property on the market just a few weeks after the contest. I heard they got back what they put into the project tenfold. I think the exposure from the project, in addition to getting first place, made their property even more desirable. It was instant publicity. Not a bad idea, actually."

The growing tightness in Cole's chest made him wonder if that was exactly the plan. It only made sense, especially with Kelly's comment about choosing not to renew Sophie's lease the following year. He couldn't tamp down the disappointment rising within him, though. To put in all the work and then for it to be sold to the highest bidder? Of course he knew he didn't have any real say in what happened to the land after he designed it, but he'd at least hoped the McAllisters would be the ones to enjoy it. It seemed almost silly for them not to.

"Anyway, I suppose it's really none of my business what they do with it." Derek dropped a hand onto Cole's shoulder. He stood up. "I think we're about ready to wrap up here. Tammy mentioned getting one last shot of you by the silos before heading out, but I've got to get that check to our caterer before Caroline texts me with one more reminder. I've stalled long enough. If I don't text back soon, she's going to send out a search party."

"Sounds good, Derek. Like I said before, I'm here if you need any help."

Derek deliberated for a brief moment. "Actually, do you think you might be able to grab the programs? They're just over at Fairvale Copy off Main Street. They've been paid for and everything, just need to be picked up. I hate to ask you to do it, but it would seriously be a huge help."

"I can definitely manage that," Cole said. "Where do you want me to deliver them?"

"It's probably best if you give them directly to Caroline. With my luck, I'd misplace or lose them, and I think weddings have been called off over lesser offenses."

"Consider it done."

"Thanks again, man. You're a lifesaver."

"Cole?" Tammy's voice broke into their conversation, her hollering loud and insistent from across the yard. "Cole, we're ready for you."

"Good luck, man. You're in the homestretch now."

∼

"WHAT WAS YOUR goal with these flowers? We love how you've included your very own little patch. It goes so well with the farm-like scenery. Can you tell our viewers a bit more about your decision to involve them?"

Tammy held the microphone a few inches from Cole's mouth, awaiting his answer. He swallowed so loudly, he worried the microphone picked it up.

"The flowers?"

"Yes." Tammy turned around. The cameraman followed her gaze, sweeping the lens across Sophie's two acres of blooms. "All of these amazing flowers, Cole. Where did you get the idea to create a space just for them? We've seen other landscapers use flowers throughout their design in planters and in pots more as accents, but you've created row upon row here. Would you mind telling us why you did this?"

Rubbing the back of his neck, Cole blew out a breath. "I wish I could, but I can't take credit for the flowers. They belong to a local farmer and were here before we began the backyard landscape."

"Well, I would never have known they weren't part of the project. Very well done, Cole." Tammy looked back into the lens. "That's it for today's *Backyard and Beyond Summer Showcase* tour. Stay tuned tomorrow morning for the design talents of Westwood and Sons Landscaping as they take over the Sanchez property. And don't forget, voting begins June tenth and lasts through the thirtieth. If you see a backyard you love, don't forget to cast your vote! See you right back here on Channel 12 News tomorrow morning. Stay fabulous, Fairvale!"

The camera fell away from the cameraman's face and Tammy took a step toward Cole. With a lowered voice, she said, "I'm not going to ask you who those flowers belong to, because I don't want any information that could drag me into the middle of this. I have a feeling Derek didn't mention anything earlier for that exact reason, but I suggest you work something out before voting begins so you don't get disqualified. Are we understood?"

Cole nodded. "Understood."

"It would really be a shame for all of this to blow up in your face, Cole. I've known the McAllisters for many years now, and they aren't known as the most forgiving people. If you ruin this for them, things could get ugly. Don't say I didn't warn you."

～

TAMMY'S ADMONITION REPLAYED in Cole's head as he drove to the copy shop to collect the programs. Even when he turned up the car radio to full blast, he could hear her words loud and clear over the lyrics. He was in a bind, with what seemed like no way out. Ever the bearer of bad news, he'd have to let Sophie know. There just wasn't any way around it.

He rehearsed a thousand times on the short drive, but when he knocked on the door and she greeted him on the other side of it, all of those words flew right out of his brain.

"What are you doing here, Cole?"

She wore gray sweatpants and a short-sleeved shirt that read *Garden Gal* across the front. Her hair was swept into a messy bun on top of her head and even though he could see she wasn't wearing makeup, she glowed with beauty.

Cole swallowed.

"Why are you here?" she repeated again.

"Wedding programs." He stretched out the stack of papers into the gap between them. "I picked them up for your brother and he suggested I bring them straight to Caroline so he didn't have a chance to lose them."

Sophie took them from his hands. "Dang it. These were supposed to be cut and folded." Her mouth flipped into a frown. "Never mind. It's fine. I'll fix them before Caroline gets back so she doesn't have a conniption. She's in full-on bridezilla mode."

"I could help."

Sophie's eyes rounded. "You don't have to—"

"I'm pretty good with a pair of scissors. Once had a dog grooming business back when I was ten. Cutting paper is about a thousand times easier than cutting poodle fur."

"Cole…"

"Please let me help, Sophie. I'd really like to."

She took a step back. "Fine."

They gathered two pairs of scissors from a drawer in the kitchen and then spread out the programs onto the coffee table in assembly line fashion. Sophie folded while Cole cut and before they knew it, they hit their groove. Two-hundred and fifty programs and one hand cramp later, they were finished.

"All done!" Sophie exclaimed as she folded the very last pamphlet and set it atop the pile. "Remind me not to have a big wedding. Someone has to do their part in saving the trees."

"It is a lot of paper, isn't it? Did they invite all of Fairvale?"

"Well, Caroline has never really met a stranger and Derek did invite most of his coworkers from the station."

"Speaking of the station, Tammy and her camera crew came out today to film the segment for their show. Your brother and I even had some time to chat."

Panic gripped Sophie's features. "Derek was there? Well that makes so much more sense now. I was wondering how he ended up asking you to get the programs."

"Sophie, I think you were right about all of this not working. I didn't come right out and tell her, but it's obvious Tammy knows the farm is yours."

Sophie slumped against the couch. Her eyes slipped shut as her head dropped back onto the cushion. "I'm just going to rip it all out."

"What?"

"My flowers. I'll just harvest them all early and take them to the market this week and sell what I can."

"That seems extreme."

"I don't know what else to do, Cole. Do you have another option? I can't just leave it there."

"But take them all out? Really?"

"There's nothing else to do."

"I could try to convince the McAllisters to bow out of the competition," Cole suggested.

"Oh, like that's going to happen."

"I'm serious. I have a hunch they plan to sell anyway. Maybe I can get them to put it on the market earlier."

"They're planning to sell?" Sophie's voice shot up three octaves. "That's even worse!"

"I don't know if they're going to, it's just something Derek suggested."

"Why does this always happen?"

"Why does what always happen?"

"Why am I always the last one to know anything, Cole?"

"I'm not even one-hundred percent sure there is anything to know. It just makes sense, when you think about it. That's why Kelly mentioned not renewing the lease and why they are so insistent on winning this contest. It all points to them intending to put the place on the market."

With her lips pursed together, Sophie exhaled slowly through her nose. "Did you have anything else for Caroline? Or just the programs?"

Cole took that as his sign. Uncrossing his legs, he pushed off the floor to stand. "That's it."

"I'll make sure she gets them." She glanced toward the door. Cole took the hint.

"I'll see myself out."

He hated the tension between them, their interactions strained tight as a rubber band.

Cole had his hand on the door handle.

"Cole, wait."

He whipped around.

"Thank you for bringing these over," Sophie said. "That was a nice thing to do."

"I'm here for you, Sophie. Anything you need. I'm serious."

She just nodded as he slipped out the door.

SOPHIE

"OF COURSE THERE would be a typo."

"It's not that noticeable," Derek tried to reassure his fiancé. He rubbed his hand in slow circles on her back, but Caroline shrugged away from his touch.

"Not noticeable? Derek, it says chocolate *mouse* instead of *mousse*! That's a pretty big mistake!"

"It's actually a really, really small mistake. It's only missing one letter."

"It's terrible! People are going to think we're serving chocolate dipped rodents for dessert! We have to fix this." Caroline's hand flew to her face to cover her eyes. "I knew something like this would happen. I just knew it."

"I agree with Derek; I don't think anyone will even notice." Sophie tried to console her roommate, but there wasn't any point. Caroline was in tears over the misprint. Sophie had known her friend long enough to know she just needed to cry it out and get it out of her system.

"I'll call the copier and see if we can have them

reprinted. I'm sure they'll be able to do it in time. It's only Monday."

"It cost us almost four hundred dollars to print them the first time, Derek! With the table linen issue, we're already eight hundred over budget. We can't afford to waste more money."

"Then let's just try to forget about it. As long as we don't point it out, no one will notice, sweetie. I'm sure of it."

Caroline pressed her hands to the countertop and puffed out her chest with a deep breath. "I need to get some air."

"Let's go for a walk then," Derek suggested, still trying his hardest.

"A walk would be good, but I think I should take it on my own."

Sophie could read the dejection on her brother's face. Still, he let Caroline have her space. "I'll be right here when you get back. Today and forever."

Caroline left a kiss on his cheek. "I know you will."

Once she was out the door, Derek turned to his sister. "I guess now isn't the best time to tell her Scott's not coming."

"He's not?" Sophie couldn't believe it. "Did he tell you that?"

"Gosh, no. You think he'd actually contact me to give me the news? No, I heard from Mom this morning. Said something about Aimee having her first cold and how they can't leave her with a sitter since she's sick, but I know that's not the real reason." Derek leaned against the kitchen counter and folded his arms. "I don't know why I thought he'd show. I get that we don't talk, but this is a big day."

It wasn't surprising news, but Sophie still felt bad that her brothers hadn't been able to work things out over the years. Their stubbornness earned them nothing but repeated heartache and disappointment.

"I hate to be the devil's advocate here, but you didn't make it to his wedding, either, Derek."

"I was on assignment then. You know that."

"For the Central Valley Garlic Festival. It wasn't like you were overseas or covering the presidential inauguration or anything."

"The festival is a big deal. People get really passionate about their garlic goods, Sophie. There was an all out brawl at the garlic paste tent last year."

Sophie shook her head.

"Did you just roll your eyes at me?" Derek asked.

"Sorry. Didn't mean to do that out loud," she quipped. "Listen, all I'm saying is that there are quite a few double standards here and I think if there's to be any sort of reconciliation, someone has to give. Maybe you should be the bigger person in this situation."

"Not sure I'm comfortable taking this advice from the woman who currently isn't speaking to the man she's fallen madly in love with. Hate to break it to you, sis, but pigheadedness seems to run in our family."

"I *am* speaking to him," Sophie blurted. "And I'm not madly in love with him!"

"Caroline has said otherwise. She's told me everything."

"What? I told her not to!"

"Seriously?" Derek's chin pulled back. "Did you

think I wouldn't figure it out? I get that you were trying to keep things secret so the McAllisters didn't get disqualified, but honestly, even if you and Cole were mortal enemies, it wouldn't change the fact that your farm is part of their property. I was hoping you all would work something out, sis, but you've put me in an impossible position."

"Cole has put us in an impossible position."

"How is this his fault? You knew my station was sponsoring this year. You do realize this looks bad all around, right? Even if the McAllisters aren't eliminated from the competition because we're siblings, there's no way the station would ever let them win. The whole thing would look rigged."

Sophie sighed. "I just wish they would've told me their plans to enter before I planted my entire crop. I would've done something different."

"Like what? Rented land elsewhere?"

Sophie lifted her shoulders. "Or bought something. That's always been my ultimate goal."

"And what makes you think you can't do that now?"

"What good would it do for me to buy land now, Derek? There's no way I can pay rent to the McAllisters' *and* pay a mortgage on an entirely separate piece of property that will just sit vacant until next season."

"I'm not talking about a separate piece of property. I'm talking about the McAllister property."

Sophie gaped. "You think I should try to buy the flower farm?"

"I don't think it would hurt to ask. Seems like a magical solution, if you ask me. You can keep your flowers. The McAllisters can still enter the contest. And you'd be free to fall in love with Cole, nothing standing in your way."

"I'm not falling in love with Cole."

"You're right. I suppose that's already done."

~

SOPHIE THOUGHT ON her brother's suggestion all evening, weighing the pros and cons. She even made a list and the column of reasons to buy far outweighed the column with reasons not to. But there was one hefty reason that tipped the scales: money.

She didn't have any.

Sure, she had some savings that she'd tucked away over the years, depositing bits of cash here and there when she had a little extra to spare, but when it came down to it, being a flower farmer sometimes meant living paycheck to paycheck. Or wedding to wedding and market to market in her case. Flower farming certainly wasn't a get rich quick venture.

But Derek was right. Buying the McAllister property would solve each and every problem. It would be magical, but what Sophie knew of life so far, magic only existed in fairytales.

Maybe, just maybe, that magic could exist in Fairvale.

~

SOPHIE WAS UP early the next morning. After swinging by Heirloom Coffee for a decaf lavender latte, she drove out to the farm. The sun peeked out over the low hills, streams of radiant light filling her truck with a warm, welcoming embrace from Mother Nature. The crystal cross that hung from Sophie's rearview mirror caught the light and prisms of color bounced all over the cab. Admittedly, she'd gone to bed in a sour mood, but the beautiful start to her morning couldn't be ignored.

Even a day of weeding wasn't undesirable since the weather was so perfect. In fact, it was just what she needed: to dig deep into the soil and to pull out the pesky problems by the roots. There was a satisfaction that came with clearing the garden of things that would otherwise inhibit growth. It was a necessary process and Sophie didn't mind it one bit.

She took her time driving to the farm, and when she arrived and angled her truck up along the curb next to the McAllister's gate, she didn't allow herself to become frazzled by Cole's rental car parked just a few feet away. She hadn't been mad at him, really, just frustrated by the situation. Cole was a hard person to stay mad at. Each time Sophie had resolved to be angry, she would think about their easy banter, the way he looked at her when he thought she wasn't looking, how he held her in his protective arms. And those dimples. Those dimples were her kryptonite.

She couldn't trick herself into believing that she hadn't formed deep and real feelings for Cole. Of course she had. And she had a hunch those feelings were reciprocated. But their timing had been so off. Had they met at any other time, things would've been fine. When it came down to it, that seemed to be the case for just about every relationship in Sophie's past. Maybe she was meant to be alone.

Killing the engine to her truck, she flung the door open

and startled when it knocked into a man standing at the side of the vehicle.

"I'm so sorry!" Sophie blurted.

"It's my fault," the man replied. He wore runner's shorts and a t-shirt that had sweat marks pooling around the collar and chest. "I hadn't realized anyone was in the truck."

Sophie didn't say anything.

"I'm sorry," he said, picking up on her unease. "I was just admiring it. Is it a '54?"

"Close. '53."

The man ran his hand along the hood. "My grandpa had one of these. I remember riding around with him when I was a kid. He always took me down to the ice cream shop in it, so I called it his ice cream truck."

"If only it played music like an actual ice cream truck," Sophie said, smiling. "That would be something."

"I don't know. There's not much you could do to improve a classic like this. You've done a fantastic job..." He paused.

"Sophie." She extended her hand for a shake.

"Nice to meet you, Sophie," he said, taking her hand into his. "I'm Brian." He didn't take his eyes off of the truck. "Sorry to keep you. I was just going for my morning run and when I rounded the corner and saw your truck, I just had to stop to take a look. It's a real beauty. Anyway, enjoy your day."

"Same to you."

Revving up, the man pumped his arms and jogged away.

Over the years, Sophie had been stopped on multiple occasions by people who wanted a closer look at her truck.

There was something about the vehicle that summoned a deep nostalgia. She loved that she could share that with others. In fact, back when she'd had more time, she even attended classic car shows, but in recent years she just couldn't fit those into her busy schedule.

Grabbing her weeding tools from the truck bed, Sophie slung the tote over her shoulder and walked up to the gate to punch in her code. The gate beeped twice, then swung wide open to allow her through.

Cole's crew was hard at work, men dispersed throughout the yard with shovels, clippers, and trash bags as they put the finishing touches on the landscape. In truth, Sophie couldn't believe how quickly it had all come together. That was the true marker of talent: that Cole could bring his ideas into reality so effortlessly. And despite her unsavory feelings toward Tanner, he had been the perfect lead for the project. There were many times when Sophie could hear him instructing his team. He sure didn't speak the language of love, but he was a born leader with a fire in his belly for greatness and it showed.

"Morning Sophie," Tanner said as Sophie made her way through the yard toward her flowers. He scooped a shovel full of sand from a bucket and sprinkled it over the brick pavers while another man took a broom and swept it into the cracks.

"Good morning, Tanner. Looking good out here."

"I'm looking good or the landscaping is looking good?"

"The landscaping, Tanner. The landscaping."

He shrugged. "A guy can dream."

Sophie just shook her head. Tanner needed little

encouragement and Sophie didn't wish to offer him even the smallest bit.

She glanced ahead. Her flowers looked picturesque just beyond the picket fencing. They'd grown tall over the last month, some reaching all the way to her shoulders. Opening the low gate, she stepped into her garden. Though the intent had always been to make Sophie's flower farm feel like a part of the overall property, she could see how it could easily be parceled off. After all, there was now fencing on all four sides, sectioning her two acres apart from the rest of the land. And there was a little dirt road that ran from the street back to her area, making her portion accessible without even setting foot in the McAllister backyard. She rarely took it, mostly due to the pieces of gravel that inevitably kicked up under her tires. Sure, it was a truck, but it was a classic after all, and the paint job wasn't cheap.

Maybe this could actually become hers one day. That hope didn't seem so far off when she really assessed it.

Either way, it wasn't something she could solve right then, so she reached into her tote to gather a pair of gloves. She slipped them onto her hands and got to work. The soil was cold and damp. Crouching down, Sophie crawled her way up and down the rows, leaving neat piles of weeds at the ends of each to collect when she finished.

Her zinnias were thriving. They were bright and bold, with fiery oranges and hot pinks. She had deadheaded early in the season and loved that each time she cut a flower from the plant, it made room for more to grow. The process fascinated her, how taking something away often made things stronger and healthier.

Maybe life was supposed to be the same.

The thought of Cole going back to Nashville wasn't a welcome one. But Sophie just didn't see any other ending. Every time she played things out between them, the end result was always the same: they would go back to their separate lives, like nothing had ever happened.

Several hours passed before Sophie became aware of the ache in her shoulders and stinging tingle of her legs beginning to fall asleep. Stretching upward, she stood tall. When her eyes met Cole's, she nearly screamed.

"I'm so sorry!" he blurted. A single row of zinnias separated them. "I didn't mean to scare you, Soph."

"How long have you been there?"

"Not very. Tanner said you got here a couple of hours ago, but I've been inside with Kelly going over the final bill." He adjusted his glasses. "It did take me a while to find you among all of these flowers, though. Seriously, Soph. There are thousands."

"Something around there."

"You can't just pull them all out. That would be a monumental waste."

"I'm not going to pull them out."

Cole smiled, those two dimples settling into his cheeks. Sophie forced herself not to look at them. "That's good news. I thought you probably said that in haste."

"If you hadn't realized already, I tend to say a lot of things in haste."

"No, you're kidding," he said so sarcastically Sophie could physically feel the words.

"I know. Shocker, right?"

He chuckled. "Are you planning to harvest for tonight's market?"

"As soon as I get the weeding done. That's my goal."

"Let me help you."

"That seems to be your standard request lately. Asking if you can help me. With the programs. Now the flowers."

"If you haven't noticed, I like being around you, Soph. If I can use helping as an excuse, then I'm going to use it."

Sophie could feel her cheeks warm. Cole was direct and she appreciated that, but she didn't want to encourage something that could never come to fruition. Even still, she did need the help. Turning him down didn't feel like the smartest option.

"I *could* use the help."

"Then put me to work. Do I just start cutting? Hacking here and there willy-nilly?"

"No!" she shouted. "I mean, no. There's a specific way each variety needs to be harvested. We'll start with the zinnias. Grab a pair of shears over in that garden tote?"

Cole walked down the row to Sophie's flower printed tote and pulled out a pair of clippers. He opened and closed them a few times in his grip before meeting her back in the middle of the row.

"Okay, so see this flower?" She took hold of the stem on one of her State Fair zinnias. "It looks like it's ready to harvest, right?"

"Yeah."

Waggling the stem back and forth, the flower head flopped around like it was attached to a wet noodle. "But see how wobbly it is? That means it's not quite ready, even though it looks like it is. You want to harvest the flowers that stand stick straight when you wiggle their stems." She took hold of another flower on the same plant. "Like this one." When she shook the stem, the neck didn't move. "Now you try it."

Cole took a stem and shook it. The zinnia swayed back and forth with bendy movements. "Looks good to me." He opened the clippers, ready to snip.

"No!" Sophie grabbed ahold of his hand in panic. "That one's not ready." Then, taking his other free hand, she placed it on a stem and wrapped her hand over his. She moved it back and forth with deliberate motions so he could really get a feel for it. "See how this one is more rigid and doesn't bend at the neck like the other one? That's what we're looking for."

Beaming, Cole laughed. "I know. I just wanted you to hold my hand."

Sophie's mouth went dry.

"But I think you should show me again because I'm a really slow learner."

16

COLE

*T*HEY HARVESTED NINE buckets of flowers in the span of an hour and a half. Once they had finished with the zinnias, they moved on to the bachelor's buttons and gomphrena. Sophie carefully instructed how to cut each one. Cole loved the passion in her tone, her eyes, and her movements when she was in the garden. Without question, this was her happy place. The thought of it being sold off left a sick taste in Cole's mouth.

He hadn't outright asked Kelly if they were going to sell, but he didn't need to. The collection of realtor business cards on the kitchen island was all the confirmation he needed.

He would tell Sophie, when the time was right.

For now, he wanted to savor each moment in her flower field with her.

"How many more do you need for tonight's market?"

"This should be enough. I'm planning to just sell single stems since I don't have time to make arrangements."

"I can help you make some if you want."

"There you go again, always offering to help."

Cole cocked his head to the side. "Would you rather I didn't help you?"

"No. Not at all. I really do appreciate it. And the company is nice."

"That, I can agree with."

Cole couldn't help it. He was falling for this woman. Sure, she was feisty and at times even combative, but Cole knew it was only out of need to protect herself. Didn't she realize he wanted to be the one to protect her?

"Plus, bouquet making is a whole different skillset," Sophie added.

Cole grinned. "Why don't you let me try?"

"To make a bouquet?"

"Yeah? Why not? You got an empty vase around here somewhere?"

Sophie nodded toward a white shed at the back of the plot. "There should be a few Mason jars stored in there. You can go ahead and grab one if you like."

Cole jogged over to the structure. It was small, probably only four by six feet or so. He tugged on the handle and opened the door. The smell of damp earth hit him. Shovels and rakes lined the walls and a paint-chipped garden stool sat in the corner. There were bags of potting soil and a crate with open seed packets, their corners ripped off and tops folded, left over from a previous planting. Just to the right, Cole spotted two empty Mason jars on the ground. He hurried back toward Sophie and held one out for her.

"How about you make one and I'll make one and we'll see whose is best?"

"You certainly have a competitive streak, don't you, Cole?"

"Considering I grew up playing nothing but sports—and the entire reason I came out to California was to participate in a competition—I would say this shouldn't come as much of a surprise."

"I'm not surprised." She laughed and reached out for a garden hose at her feet. "Hold out your jar and I'll fill it up."

Grabbing the nozzle, Sophie squeezed. Water shot from the spout with the force of a fire hose. Cole's jar clattered to the ground, breaking at his feet. The hose handle stuck and blasts of freezing water sprayed into the air as Sophie attempted to wrangle the line.

Through the deluge, Cole couldn't see through his glasses and had to feel his way about. Inadvertently, he smacked the hose from Sophie's hands, but it continued writhing along the ground, like a maniacal snake chasing after its prey.

"Grab it!" Sophie squealed. Water showered down over them with the intensity of a desert monsoon. "Grab it, Cole!"

"I'm trying!" he said, but the rush of water hindered everything, including his vision. "What the heck is wrong with this hose?"

"It's done this before," Sophie shouted over the commotion. "It's like it has a mind of its own!"

Cole bent down, sweeping his hands along the ground as water sprayed onto his face. Suddenly, he felt an object and wrapped his hand around it, but the sharp sting that came along with it indicated he'd grabbed the wrong thing. His palm burned and warm liquid ran over his skin.

"Shoot."

"What happened?"

"Nothing," Cole lied. "I'm fine."

Then, finally, he stepped on the defiant hose, temporarily cutting off the water supply. The nozzle fell to the ground like a popped balloon dropping out of the sky.

Sophie retrieved it and twisted the nozzle off. She blew out a breath of relief, but then a look of shock flashed across her face. "Cole! You're bleeding!"

"What?" He looked down at his hand, at the scarlet red that painted his palm. "Oh, I guess I am. I must've cut it on the jar when I was trying to get hold of that possessed garden hose."

"That looks really bad." Rushing forward, Sophie pulled his hand into hers. Water droplets clung to her eyelashes and beaded on her skin. Her shirt was just as soaked as Cole's, like she had jumped into a pool fully clothed. "You might need stitches."

"I don't need stitches." He wasn't certain about that, but that was always the answer when someone suggested stitches. Needles were not his friend. He pulled his glasses from his face and wiped them with his shirt before settling them back onto his nose. "I'm fine."

"It looks really deep."

It did. The cut was long and clean, causing his skin to separate straight across the center of his hand, like he had been filleted.

"Here, this might help." Reaching up, Sophie pulled the blue bandana from her hair. She held Cole's hand face-up, and wound the fabric around twice before securing it tightly in a knot across his palm. She curled his fingers protectively over it. "This is only temporary. You're going to need to go to a doctor."

"I think this will be just fine, Nurse Sophie."

"Cole, I'm being serious. That's a really deep flesh wound. I could almost see muscle."

Cole staggered forward. A black haze blurred the edges of his vision, like the static on a television screen.

Sophie caught him by his shoulders. "Whoa there, Cole. You look really pale. You need to sit down."

He tried to take a step forward, but everything swayed around him. The buzzing of a thousand bees filled his ears.

Sophie grabbed a bucket filled with just-picked flowers, dumped them onto the sodden ground, and flipped it over. "Sit," she commanded.

Cole dropped down onto the bucket. His stomach lurched and he swallowed hard.

"Breathe, Cole. In through your nose, out through your mouth." Sophie demonstrated the forced, intentional breaths. Inhale, exhale. Inhale, exhale.

Cole followed her instructions, pinching his eyes shut.

Crouching down between his feet, Sophie placed her hands on Cole's knees and looked up at him with pleading eyes. "Put your head between your knees and relax, Cole. You're going to be just fine."

He did so and slowly the buzzing began to subside. When he lifted back up and pried his eyes open, the black edges were gone. Everything snapped into focus.

He was humiliated.

"I'm so sorry."

Sophie's eyebrows scrunched together. "Why on earth are you apologizing?"

"Because I almost passed out."

"That doesn't require an apology, Cole. Lots of people get squeamish at the sight of blood."

Cole clamped his eyes shut again and breathed in sharply through his nose. "I know. I just feel stupid."

"The only reason you should feel stupid is because you look absolutely ridiculous. Like you dove into an ocean."

"You look just the same," Cole retorted. "But I wouldn't say you look ridiculous at all. You always look beautiful to me."

Sophie's mouth fell open. "Cole..." She started, but her words trailed off. Her hands were still on his knees, and despite the chill from his wet clothes, he felt warmth where her palms rested. "Cole, I..."

"What?" Cole's voice cracked with the syllable.

His gaze stayed fixed on her mouth, hoping he could draw the words from her. Her tongue swept across her bottom lip.

"I..."

Cole leaned forward. Sophie pushed up onto her knees.

Reaching out, Cole placed his good hand on the back of Sophie's head and drew her closer. Her eyes flitted back and forth between his. He could feel her breath on his skin and his pulse spiked. When her hand lifted to his jaw, he exhaled, dizzied once again, but for an entirely different reason.

His heart caught in his throat. "I really want to kiss you right now, Sophie."

She pressed her lips to his. They were sudden and soft and insistent all at once. Cole wove his arm around her waist and held her to his body as their mouths met. The heartbeat that had buzzed so loudly earlier now thrummed in his neck, his chest, his ears. He played with her hair, weaving the damp strands between his fingers. A sigh escaped her as she drew back, and then Sophie pressed in, her hands moving across his shoulders to his back as she tugged him closer.

"This flower field is part of the property," a muffled woman's voice said in the distance. "I think we should include it in the overall asking price, but it can be parceled off easily, as well."

Sophie shot back on her haunches, her eyes wild. Cole dropped his hands from her hair.

"This would be the perfect spot for a pool. Many buyers are specifically looking for homes with pools, especially with our hot California summers. Do you happen to know how big this space is?"

"Just shy of two acres, I believe."

Gulping, Sophie leaned in and whispered, "Is that Kelly?"

"I think so," Cole murmured back. He pushed up a little to look over the tops of the flowers. Sophie yanked him back down.

"Don't let her see you," she hissed. "Who is she talking to?"

"My best guess would be a realtor." At those words, Sophie's face paled. "Sophie." He reached out.

"No. It's fine, Cole."

"It's not."

The voices of the two women trailed off as they made their way back into the house. Sophie tossed her head. "It is what it is."

"I'm going to figure out a way this land can be yours."

"It's not your responsibility to do that, Cole. I'm a big girl. I can take care of myself."

"But I want to take care of you."

Her eyes went wide. "Cole—"

"Let me take care of you, Sophie."

Leaning close, Cole pressed his mouth to Sophie's again. Cole cupped her jaw and kissed her with everything he had. It was sweet yet desperate, this mix of emotion that seemed to sum up their entire relationship.

As they stayed hidden among the flowers, their lips confessing every unspoken feeling and thought, Cole knew without a doubt he'd never be able to go back to Nashville. Not now.

There was no way he could leave this woman.

If he did, he would be leaving his entire heart behind.

~

THE MARKET THAT night was even busier than the last. Cole noticed several new vendors and how the tents were set even closer together, leaving very little space to move around between them. Everywhere he looked, he saw mounds of colorful fruits and vegetables, displays of housewares, and racks of homemade creations. It was a visual feast.

Sophie was remarkable. Her ability to organize something so integral to the community made Cole swell with pride. He loved this about her the most: her determined spirit and go-getter attitude. It made him wonder if he had misspoken when he said he'd wanted to take care of her. She was self-sufficient; that was a quality he greatly admired in her. But even the most independent people needed someone to care for them. Love and independence weren't mutually exclusive.

At Sophie's urging, Cole had gone to Urgent Care after he left the McAllister's. She had been right. He did need stitches. He'd turned green and nearly became sick in the wastebasket, but he toughed it out. The doctor had wrapped a bandage around his hand and instructed him to leave it on for the next couple of days. Luckily, it had been Cole's left hand, so it didn't inhibit him too much, but there was an obvious inconvenience associated with it. Even still, despite the pain and the nausea, this day had been one of his best.

Cole had wanted to kiss Sophie for over a month. It wasn't at all how he'd pictured it taking place, and that was what made it so wonderful. In that moment in the flowers with her, he couldn't think of anything he would rather do, or anyone he would rather be with.

And the kiss itself. It was fair to say Sophie had ruined him for all others.

Cole was on cloud nine as he strolled the market rows. Jerry Potters was the musical talent for the night, and that helped to shave off a bit of the jealousy Cole would have experienced had Sophie hired other talent. Plus, it was fun to listen to her dad jam on his guitar. He had said before that it had been years since he'd held one in his hands, but that was hard to believe. Jerry was a musician through and through and the crowd that gathered around to appreciate his music evidenced that.

Just like previous markets, this was a town celebration.

"Hey, lover boy." Jolting, Cole turned around and locked eyes with Veronica. She wore a long bohemian dress and had her hair done in a single black braid that trailed down her back. "Looking for Sophie?"

"No. I mean, it's not that I'm not looking for her, I

just…" Cole's words tangled. "Do you know where she is?"

"That's what I thought. Man, you two are sure hot and cold, aren't you, sweets?"

"I wouldn't say that. I think things are just complicated at the moment."

"Well, that sounds incredibly tongue twisted," Veronica said. "Speaking of, I hear you two did the same. Locked lips, didn't you?"

Cole's stomach warmed. "Did she tell you?"

"Nope." Bopping her finger on Cole's nose like he was a child, Veronica said, "But you just did."

Veronica practically skated back to her flower tent. That's when Cole spotted Sophie. She wore cut off denim shorts and a white linen shirt tied at the waist and her hair was pulled up into a ponytail at the back of her head. She looked like summer and sunshine.

Catching his eye, her lips lifted into a smile. "Hi," she mouthed.

"Hi," Cole mouthed right back.

Crowds swarmed between them, but their gazes remained locked. Cole hadn't felt this lovesick since he was a teenager. He had missed the nervous excitement that went hand in hand with falling for someone. It was exhilarating and thrilling, with equal amounts of anxiety sprinkled in.

He made his way over to her.

"Hi," he said again, this time audibly. He leaned in for a kiss, but Sophie pulled back.

"Not here," she whispered, her eyes darting side to side like she'd been caught cheating on a test. "Not that I don't want to."

"It was pretty amazing, right?"

Cole noticed the rosy glow that spread onto Sophie's cheeks. "It was."

"Actually, I think I'm starting to forget just how amazing it was. I need a refresher."

"Later," Sophie said. She placed a palm on Cole's chest and pushed him back. Then, looking down at his hand, she shouted, "You did listen to me!"

"Of course I did."

"And what did the doctor say? Did you get stitches?"

Cole's mouth flipped into a frown. "I did. Seven, to be exact."

"Ouch. I'm so sorry, Cole. What a complete mess this morning turned out to be."

"I wouldn't say that at all. I think it was perfect."

Sophie shrugged. "It's too bad about your hand because my dad was asking if you might want to accompany him tonight. I told him about your accident and that you probably wouldn't be able to play."

"My hand might be busted, but my voice isn't. I can join him for backup vocals for few songs if he wants. I'd be happy to." Then, smirking, Cole added, "And my lips are working just fine, too, I'll have you know."

Sophie shoved Cole playfully. "Don't tempt me. I'm technically working here."

"Rain check, then?"

"Deal." Sophie said, offering the sweetest grin.

17

SOPHIE

*T*HAT KISS HAD rocked Sophie's world. She had a feeling it would, which was probably the reason why she'd held off so long in making that move. But in that moment, there was nothing she could think to do but to kiss Cole. It was as though all of the earth's magnetic force was fixed on them, drawing them toward one another. In her twenty-seven years, Sophie had kissed several men, but nothing even remotely compared to that kiss with Cole.

So why did he have to be from Tennessee while Sophie was a California girl through and through? While they were so drawn toward one another, their lives would eventually pull them apart. Was it wise to give her heart over to someone who would end up taking it across the country with them? Sophie would never leave California. This was her home. Her roots were deep and established here. But Cole's business and his future were in Nashville. That was the truth of it all. They both knew it.

Sophie honestly didn't know what to do.

"What's up, buttercup?" Veronica elbowed her friend. "You seem distant today."

"Do I?" Sophie snapped from her wandering thoughts. "I've just got a lot on my mind, I suppose."

From the other side of the table, a woman holding a baby on her hip pointed to a bucket of Benary's Giant zinnias. "How much?"

"Fifty cents a stem or a dozen for five dollars," Sophie answered, then turned back to Veronica. She lowered her voice to barely above a whisper. "Cole and I kissed."

"I know. He told me."

"Wait, what? He told you? When?"

"Well, he didn't so much tell me as confirm what I already knew to be true. That man is smitten, doll. It's plain as day."

"It was amazing, Ver. Like life-altering type of amazing."

"Okay, now you're just bragging."

Sophie sighed. "I haven't felt like this about anyone before. It's kind of scary."

"Nothing to be afraid of. What's the worst that can happen?"

"I could have my heart broken."

"A broken heart just means that you've let yourself love, and that's the greatest thing we can do while on this round, spinning thing we call earth."

"I'll take these, please." Another customer lifted up a fistful of flowers to pass to Sophie. "My wife will just love them." He held out a ten-dollar bill in the other hand and offered a genial smile while he waited for her response.

"I'll get those wrapped up for you." Sophie took the bouquet and settled the flowers down on a sheet of brown

Kraft paper. She turned toward Veronica, continuing the sidebar conversation at a lowered volume. Not all of Fairvale needed to know about her romantic woes. "I don't want a broken heart."

"So you don't want to fall in love—that's what you're getting at?"

"I didn't say that." She measured and snipped twine to tie around the bouquet.

"Yes, you did. Love involves heartache, even in the best of scenarios. Happily ever after isn't real, doll. Even the most solid relationships will go through hardships and trying times. What you're telling me is that you want a fairytale that doesn't exist."

Passing the bouquet back to the gentleman across the folding table, Sophie smiled. "I hope your wife likes them. Be sure to change their water every couple of days and you should get a good two weeks' worth of enjoyment out of them." Then she said to Veronica, "I'm saying I don't want to dive into anything that is going to end up in certain heartbreak. That doesn't seem unreasonable."

"It's totally unreasonable. Life isn't all puppies and flowers." Veronica paused. "Okay, maybe it *is* all flowers for us, but you know what I mean. Let yourself fall for him, Sophie. Even if it doesn't last. Better —"

"To have loved and lost than never to have loved at all. I know, I know."

"I was actually going to say better get a piece of that hottie before someone else snags him."

A laugh fell from Sophie's lips. "I'm going to go make the rounds while there's a lull here. Mind keeping an eye on the flowers while I'm gone?"

"Sure thing. Happy to."

Reaching under the table, Sophie fished around for her canvas tote bag and once found, slipped it onto her shoulder. She had plans to buy a pound of peaches from the Nicholson's farm for a cobbler recipe she'd discovered in a magazine last summer. She couldn't wait to test it out. Caroline was the baker in the household, but Sophie still liked to try new recipes when she stumbled upon a promising one. Maybe she would even see if Cole wanted to come over and join her for dessert that evening. Would that come across as too assertive? Was there some sort of period of time after a kiss that one was supposed to wait until planning another? It wasn't like she was planning another kiss, necessarily, though she did suppose she had promised Cole one.

"Hello, Miss Potters." The same voice that had caught her so off guard earlier that day in the flowers now made her stomach bottom out.

"Kelly." Sophie ran a hand through her bangs, shoving her hair out of her eyes. "How are you?"

"I'm well, thank you. Just checking out the market. Looks like you've done a nice job recruiting vendors this year. There are so many, it's almost overwhelming."

"Honestly, after last year's success, it was pretty easy to find vendors who wanted to participate. I've even had to turn away a few due to lack of space."

"Good problem to have, I suppose." Kelly was prim and proper as always, her hair styled just so and her tailored gray dress hugging her slender body. "I've been meaning to chat with you, actually."

Those words made goose bumps rise on Sophie's skin. "You have?"

"Yes. Is there any chance you might be able to drop by the house tomorrow, say, around noon?"

"I'll already be out at the farm harvesting, so that will be no problem at all."

Kelly's head lifted in a slow, approving nod, even though she appeared to be looking down her nose at Sophie. "Great. I will plan to see you then."

"Wait!" Sophie blurted, just as Kelly turned on her heel to go. "Any chance you have some time this evening? I'm making a peach cobbler and I'd love to bring it over."

Eyes narrowing, she gave Sophie a scrutinizing once over. "This is more of a business meeting than a social activity, Sophie."

"I know. I just...well, I just figured conversation is always better when food is involved. And food is always better when it's right out of the oven. I'd hate for a piping hot cobbler to go to waste. I certainly can't eat it all by myself."

Kelly deliberated like the decision was a big one. "Okay. Fine. What time does the market finish up?"

"I'm usually home by seven. I'll get the cobbler started and in the oven right away and can be at your place by 8:30. If that's not too late for you, that is."

"That will be just fine. I will see you then."

It took Sophie several minutes to recover from the conversation, her composure rattled. Why she had forced a peach cobbler on Kelly McAllister, she had no clue. In reality, the thought of waiting until the next day to learn what Kelly wanted to talk about would just about do her in. She'd likely have a fitful night of sleep, making her a mess the following morning. Any coping skills would be out the window, and she worried if Kelly had unfavorable news, Sophie would wear her disappointment all over her face. At least if she broke it to Sophie tonight, she'd have a delicious dessert to drown her sorrows in.

"Peaches, peaches. Where are the peaches?" Sophie muttered under her breath as she scanned the market for the Nicholson's pop up tent. At one point, she had memorized the location of all of her vendors, but chatting with Kelly had turned her all kinds of confused. "There they are!"

Across the lot and next to the soy candle display was her friend's produce tent. She was glad to see plenty of stone fruit to choose from.

"Well, if it isn't Sophie Potters! Good to see you. I figured you'd be busy with your flowers all evening. The crowds tonight must be record setting. Seems like all of Fairvale is out here," Kent Nicholson said, tipping his straw hat. He was the quintessential farmer donned in denim overalls with work gloves hanging out of his back pocket. His skin was leathery, darkened from years spent under the sun, which made him look significantly older than Sophie knew him to be. Those extra wrinkles just made the friendly sparkle of his eye all the more noticeable. Kent was an endearing man, and had always been a huge supporter of Sophie's farm, a mentor of sorts when she was just getting things off the ground.

"What can I get for you tonight, my friend? Our yellow freestones are ripe right now. So sweet, they taste like candy."

Using a paring knife, Kent sliced off a peach wedge and held it out to Sophie to try.

She popped it into her mouth. Immediately, her taste buds perked up as the sweet juices coated her tongue.

"How is it possible that these are even better than last year, Kent? Are you sprinkling actual sugar on your trees?"

He chuckled. "Some years you just get doubly blessed; that's my only explanation. The valley sweets are my personal favorite, but we've already sold out of them for the evening. It's a good time to be a Fairvale farmer, isn't it?"

"It sure is," she agreed. "I'll take a pound of freestones."

"Coming right up."

While Kent weighed the peaches on a hanging scale, Sophie looked around. Just a few tents over, she could see her dad and Cole seated on two barstools while they took a break from singing. They were chuckling about something and even though Sophie couldn't hear them, she noticed Cole pull his glasses from his face and wipe his eyes with the back of his hand, as though whatever they had been talking about sent him into a fit of laughter. Her dad slapped a friendly palm between Cole's shoulder blades.

It was clear Sophie wasn't the only one who would miss Cole when he left for Nashville.

"Here you go, Sophie. One pound of freestones. Mind me asking what you plan to use them for?"

"A cobbler." She fished in her pocket for her money, but Kent held up a hand.

"Are you planning to share that cobbler with anyone?"

"Actually, I am."

"Then the peaches are on me."

Sophie shook her head. "I couldn't let you do that."

"You'll have to."

"Kent."

He wasn't about to budge. "No negotiating, Sophie.

179

I'm happy to share my bounty if I know you'll be sharing it, too. A pay it forward sort of thing. All I ask is that you give every bit of it away. Don't let any go to waste."

"I think I can handle that." She vacillated. "Are you sure I can't pay you?"

"I'm sure you *can* pay me. But I won't accept it. Enjoy that cobbler, friend."

～

EVEN WITH OVEN mitts on, the heat from the glass dish warmed Sophie's fingers, to the point that if Kelly didn't open the door soon, she would have to set the cobbler down on the front stoop to keep from burning herself.

Sophie used her elbow to press the doorbell once more.

"Kelly! Are you expecting someone?" a hoarse voice echoed through the closed door. Sophie had met Theodore McAllister on several occasions over the years, but all business dealings were typically executed with Kelly. Sophie wasn't sure why she hadn't expected Theodore to be present that evening, but the thought of him sitting in on their conversation had her reeling with panic.

"The flower girl is stopping by," she could hear Kelly answer from within the home.

Sophie had been called a lot of things over the years, but flower girl was a first.

As the bolt turned over, Sophie straightened her spine to stand tall.

"Hello there, Miss Potters. What brings you by at this hour?" Theodore was a short man with a thick voice that sounded like he'd swallowed a handful of gravel.

"Kelly said she had some things she hoped to discuss

with me." Sophie pushed the dessert out. "And I brought a peach cobbler."

"Well, why didn't you say so?" Theodore teased as he held out a hand to welcome Sophie into the house. "Come on in. Let me take that from you."

"It's hot."

"Oh, I can handle it."

Just then, Kelly came into the foyer, her lips drawn tight as she took Sophie in. She was a difficult woman to read—not unfriendly per se, just not overly warm.

"Hello there, Sophie."

"Kelly." Sophie stuck her oven mitt-clad hand out, only realizing her gaffe when Kelly's eyes narrowed. Lifting the mitt to her face, Sophie pulled it off with her teeth and held out her hand again for a shake. Hesitantly, Kelly took it.

"Let's take a seat in the family room, shall we?"

Theodore was already at work in the kitchen, dishing up heaping portions of cobbler. Steam rose from the plates in wispy curls. It made the entire home smell like a fragrant orchard in the throes of harvest season. It would be Sophie's little secret that she'd enlisted Caroline's help to make it. After she had to scrap the burned first attempt, her roommate came to her rescue. That was a huge blessing. She wouldn't be doing herself any favors by bringing an inedible dessert to a meeting that had the potential to change her future.

"This smells wonderful, Sophie," Theodore said as he passed out three plates. He offered a fork for her to take. "You're a woman of many talents, I see."

"That's very kind of you to say," Sophie replied, keeping her little culinary secret to herself. She placed the oven mitts on the coffee table and settled into the plush couch cushions. "I hope you know how grateful I am to you both for letting me farm the land these past five years. I don't know what I would do if I didn't have access to this space. Your generosity has let me live out my dreams; I hope you know that." Like she was spreading frosting on a cake, she laid the guilt on thick.

Kelly folded her hands in her lap and looked down at them. "Yes, well, that's what I wanted to talk with you about."

From his stuffed leather chair, Theodore inhaled the cobbler like it was his last meal. He made appreciative little sounds with each bite. "This is hands-down the best cobbler I've ever had. Even better than my Grandma Gertie's." Kelly's eyes cut to her husband, but he didn't pick up on her warning glare. "Any chance you can start paying your rent in dessert rather than cash?"

"He's obviously joking."

"Obviously," Sophie said.

"Speak for yourself," Theodore mumbled around a mouthful of peaches.

Kelly cleared her throat. "Anyway. Something has recently come up regarding the land and I wanted you to be the first to know."

That was a lie. Sophie was never the first to know anything when it came to the farm.

"We're planning to sell, Sophie."

With surprising control, Sophie kept her features neutral. "For how much?"

"We're not just selling your flower portion. We're selling it all. The house. The land. All of it."

"But we *can* sell just her portion, Kel."

Tightening her lips, Kelly scowled at Theodore in an attempt to silence the man, but he was so engrossed in his food that he didn't notice.

"Seriously, this is so good. Best cobbler I've ever had. I'm going to have seconds." He stood up from his seat. "Can I get anyone else another helping?"

"I'm fine, thank you," Sophie said.

"Like I was saying, we're planning to sell it all. Theodore has a job transfer to Arizona and we'll be moving in the middle of July."

"Moving at the hottest time of year to one of the hottest states in the country. We must be crazy," Theodore hollered from the kitchen.

"I know your flower season will still be going on, so I hoped to give you some advance notice so you can figure out what to do. I'm not sure, but maybe you can transplant them somewhere else?"

Sophie's stomach rolled.

"She can't transplant them, Kel. That's not how it works. There are thousands of flowers. Have you even looked at them lately? There's a whole sea of them."

"Yes. The realtor and I have looked quite closely at them. Honestly, I am just giving Sophie a heads up as a courtesy. It's well within our rights to have the lease terminated at any given point in time."

Sophie didn't know if that was true or not, but even if she wanted to challenge Kelly, she couldn't find the right words.

"I hope this doesn't come too far out of left field for you."

"Actually, it doesn't. I had a feeling something like this was on the horizon."

"Good. I don't see why we can't leave things on pleasant terms, then."

Sophie swallowed. "I do have one question, though."

"Of course."

"Why did you decide to enter the competition if you knew you would be selling?"

Kelly nodded, like the question was one she had anticipated. "At first, we didn't know we would sell. But once Theodore got the job offer and we made up our minds to relocate, we saw how winning the competition could actually help with the sale of the home."

"But you haven't even officially won yet."

"No," Kelly said. "But I've checked out the competition and there's no doubt in my mind that we will."

"You are aware that my brother is Derek Potters, right?" It was a Hail Mary that could go one of two ways. Sophie hoped it wouldn't backfire on her, but she was left with no other option.

"The local news anchor? I suppose I knew that. Yes."

"So then you're aware that this whole thing is and has been a glaring conflict of interest from the very beginning since they are sponsoring the contest. Have you considered pulling out of it completely? Especially with plans to sell, it might be best to avoid any negative press altogether."

Kelly's penciled eyebrows pulled together. "Well, I suppose it *could* be considered a conflict of interest." She stopped, then concluded, "I guess that just means we'll have to end your lease even sooner."

"Kelly." Theodore's voice was stern, even through the forkful of cobbler.

"What, Theodore? We've spent all of this money and

come all of this way. It seems like a simple solution. The only solution, really."

"I think you need more cobbler."

"I don't need more of anything. Just an understanding on Sophie's part that, as of this moment, her lease is terminated."

The room became quiet, save for the quivering breath that Sophie tried to rally into submission. She would keep it together, no matter the cost.

"That's crazy. We're not terminating her lease."

"Theo."

"I'm serious, Kel. Winning a contest is not worth losing our integrity."

"It's not about integrity, Theo. It's about being financially opportunistic. This contest will be great exposure. We'll have a bidding war for the property once it's on the market, no doubt in my mind."

"I'm not concerned about a bidding war, Kelly. We're not breaking the lease."

Kelly's hands flew up. "Then it sounds like we'll have to pull out of the competition like Sophie said! Is that what you want? You're leaving us with that as the only option."

"It's not our *only* option."

Sophie kept silent as Theodore and Kelly volleyed back and forth.

"What do you suggest, then?"

"That we sell Sophie her land," Theodore replied.

"We can't do that!"

"Of course we can. You and I both know we all but completed the process to split it into two parcels years ago when we thought your mother was interested in building on it. It's the whole reason we divvied off that particular portion for Sophie in the first place. I've got a few friends down at the county who can help expedite the whole thing and get it all signed off in no time. If Sophie buys it, then everyone wins."

Kelly wove her arms tightly over her chest as she glowered at her husband.

Just a glimmer of hope opened up within Sophie, but it was too early to let it fully unfurl.

"Give me one good reason why we wouldn't do this?"

"Because we would be losing out on that money in the overall sale. People want land, Theo. Lots of land."

"And they'll still get it. Five acres worth."

"And what? We just take what the flower farm is worth out of the asking price?"

Nodding, Theodore said, "That's exactly what we'll do."

"That doesn't seem like the smartest move, money-wise."

"Maybe not, but it feels like the best move, character-wise."

Still frowning, Kelly rolled her eyes. "Fine, do whatever you want. But that land isn't cheap, I hope you understand that, Sophie. We won't be giving it away."

"I'm prepared to pay whatever you ask."

Kelly stood and walked over to a secretary desk in the corner of the room and tore a sheet of paper off of a notepad. With a pen, she scribbled something onto the parchment and then walked over to hand it to Sophie.

Sophie unfolded the paper and gulped. She had never seen so many zeroes all lined up next to one another.

"I can make that work."

Theodore snatched the paper from Sophie's hands. "That's actually not right. It's not quite enough."

Sophie's pulse spiked. She couldn't afford to pay more than Kelly had already asked. Even that would take a small miracle.

"Add three peach cobblers to that total," Theodore said as he reached out his hand to shake Sophie's.

Grinning ear to ear, Sophie took it, sealing the deal.

COLE

*T*HE WHEELS OF the hatchback rubbed along the curb as Cole put his rental car in park in front of the McAllister property. Up ahead, he could see Sophie leaning against her truck, speaking to a man decked in full running gear. Cole had noticed the same man on multiple occasions when driving throughout Fairvale and figured he was preparing for a marathon. Rain or shine, he ran through town with determined and purposeful strides.

Cole had always been athletic, but running wasn't his thing. He wondered if it was something Sophie enjoyed. Maybe she was discussing a common interest with the stranger now. There was still so much to learn about the woman he had fallen for and the few short weeks they had left together didn't seem long enough to explore all that Cole hoped to. He needed more time.

Shutting off the engine, Cole stepped out of the car. Sophie spotted him and offered a friendly wave, even though she was deep in conversation. He nodded his hello and then walked to the gate to punch in his code. This was his favorite moment, when the gate would swing wide and the entirety of landscape came into view. It was like an unveiling. A ribbon cutting. Cole took so much pride in this finished project.

Over the last month, he had sent snapshots to his father as updates on the progress, but nothing compared to viewing it in person. He knew his dad was busy back at home and didn't have time to sneak off to California, but Cole sure wished he could. No picture would do it justice. That was the very reason they opened up the properties for tours during the voting period. The showcase had hired a professional photographer and posted images online, but the true magic was in strolling the gardens, the pathways, and the scenery. Experiencing it firsthand was so much better than viewing it on a screen.

"Mornin'!" Tanner called out from above a row of newly-planted photinia. He had long trimmers in his hands and dirt up to his elbows. "Just finishing up some last minute pruning. Also, I tightened that wobbly board on the pergola we were talking about yesterday. Gonna give it one more coat of stain before the end of the day. Should have everything buttoned up by early tomorrow morning."

"That's fantastic, Tanner. I really do appreciate all of your help on this. You and your crew worked so hard and it shows."

"It's been a great project to be a part of. I sorta wish you weren't heading back to Nashville next month—it would be fun to work with you on a few more like this."

"Truthfully, I wish I wasn't heading back, too. It's beginning to feel like there's more for me in California than at home at this point."

"You mean in the form of work?" Tanner smirked. "Or women?"

"I'd be lying if I said Sophie wasn't a huge factor in why I'm seriously considering putting down some roots here. But we haven't even talked about what the future holds for us. It's probably a bit premature for me to think about completely relocating."

"Just my two cents, but if this contest goes the way we hope it will, you'll have no problem finding consistent work out here. That, and the fact that you've already got a girl makes it seem like a no-brainer. But that's just my humble opinion, for what it's worth."

Cole didn't disagree. Fairvale would be a hard place to leave when the time came.

"I'm heading to the flowers, but I'll catch up with you in a bit. Let me know if you need anything in the meantime. It's looking great, Tanner."

Tanner saluted with a flick of his wrist. "You got it, boss."

Cole retreated to the back of the lot and threaded his way through the rows, up and down and back and forth, like winding through an autumn corn maze.

"Looking for something?" Sophie's cheery voice broke into the crisp morning air. She marched down the row toward him, her smile growing wider with each step.

"Hey there." Cole turned and drew her into a hug. He held her close for longer than usual.

"Good morning," she said against the crook of his neck, but her voice harbored a detectable uncertainty. She pulled out from his embrace, her face angled up, her brow creased with worry. "You okay?"

"I'm better now that you're here." He kissed her hair, then let go. "Any chance I can steal a few zinnias?"

"You don't even have to steal them. I'll gladly give them to you. Any particular color?"

"Nope. Whatever you're willing to part with will be just fine."

Sophie nudged her head toward the potting shed. "Go grab some shears and we'll see if you remember anything I taught you about harvesting from the other day." She waggled her eyebrows in playful challenge.

Cole retrieved the cutters and within ten minutes, he had a handheld bouquet of zinnias, fit for a market flower stand.

"Mind telling me what you plan to do with them?" Sophie asked as she wiped the clippers on her garden apron and tucked them into the pocket. "I'm hoping I don't have any reason to be jealous," she teased through a grin.

"What are you doing for the rest of the day? If there's any chance you can clear your schedule, I'll show you exactly what they're for."

∼

THE BRINY COASTAL air rushed through the open windows as Cole's vehicle hugged tightly to the curves of Highway 1. To his left stretched miles of vast, blue Pacific Ocean, no doubt one of the world's greatest splendors. To his right was another marvel—Sophie—arguably just as breathtaking as the awe-inspiring waves that crashed against the rocky shores. Cole had to purposefully focus his gaze out the windshield, but all he wanted to do was get lost in Sophie's beauty beside him.

It had been a two-hour drive from Sacramento to the coast. They stopped in Bodega Bay at a quaint little restaurant overlook that served the freshest ocean catches. They sat at a small booth with a window view and Cole ordered a pound of Dungeness crab, happy to learn it was still in season. He couldn't contain his shock when Sophie revealed she'd never eaten the shellfish, especially considering her love of sushi. It was finally his time to teach her something and they laughed throughout their entire meal as she struggled to pull meat from the hard, shelly legs. In the end, however, she consumed even more than Cole since he was charged with cracking the crab and passing all the edible pieces her way. He didn't mind one bit, though. He was more than content to watch her enjoy it.

Their final destination was only ten minutes north of their lunchtime stop. Cole finally gained the courage to take Sophie's hand into his and wished he hadn't spent the entire first portion of the drive talking himself out of doing so. His other hand on the steering wheel had already begun to heal well, and even though it was still bandaged, he didn't think much about the subtle pain. All he could focus on was the hand in Sophie's grip. She didn't pull back like he worried she would, but instead rubbed her thumb against his skin in comforting circles. That sweet, small act brought everything home for Cole. He couldn't leave California and he couldn't leave this woman. Sitting in the car with her, hand in hand, he could glimpse their entire future together, sharing more simple but significant moments just like this one.

"Duncan's Landing," Sophie read the sign aloud as Cole flipped his turn signal. He maneuvered the car into the empty lot and slowed to a stop. "Have you been here before?"

"This particular beach? No. But this ocean? Yes. Just a different part of it," Cole said as he unclasped his seatbelt and reached into the backseat to retrieve the bouquet. He gathered a rolled up beach towel and swung his gaze Sophie's direction, locking eyes. She took the towel from him. "Sophie, I have something I need to do, and I'd really like for you to be a part of it."

"Of course," Sophie agreed without hesitation. Cole knew it was a cryptic request. Even still, he was so thankful for her company because this was something he wouldn't have the strength to do alone. He needed Sophie there more than his words could articulate.

Taking her hand more confidently this time, the two began their walk down to the beach below. Long wooden planks created stairs in the craggy hillside. With each step, Cole gripped tighter to Sophie as they descended the steep ravine. Wind, biting and sharp, cut into him. Shivering, he shrugged his shoulders to his ears, pushing the collar of his jacket up higher around his neck for warmth. He had glanced at the weather app before leaving town, but had no idea the beach would be this uncomfortably cold. It was such a stark contrast to the last time he'd gazed out at this particular body of water, back when the sun beat down in unrelenting, scorching rays. Today the layered cloud cover kept the sunshine at bay. The sky looked as though all blue pigment had been pulled out, leaving only a dull, opaque gray in its place.

Sophie trembled.

"Here," Cole said, noticing her chill. Tucking the bouquet under his arm, he took the beach towel from

Sophie and draped it over her shoulders like a shawl. "I'm sorry it's so cold."

"Pretty sure you didn't have any say in today's forecast," she joked. "I don't mind it, actually. It's invigorating. Like stepping into the cold storage room at Costco."

Cole chuckled. "It's freezing."

"Well, I suppose we'll just have to create our own warmth then," she said as she snuck her arm under his jacket to wrap around Cole's waist, drawing him close to her side.

They made their way to the cove. Sprays of water misted the air around them as wave after wave assaulted the shoreline. The white, powdery sand Cole had expected to find was nowhere to be seen. Instead, an infinite amount of fine pebbles made up the beach's grainy texture. He was utterly amazed by Northern California's rocky coast. This golden state continually took him by surprise.

"This isn't what I pictured a California beach to look like." Reaching out, Cole withdrew the towel from Sophie's shoulders and spread it onto the sand underneath them. He held her hand as she lowered to sit and then joined her there.

"You thought all of California was Southern California. Common mistake. We're not just geographically far apart—there are many, many other differences. Sure, you'll see a surfer or two out here, but they'll be in full wetsuit attire. These aren't exactly the beaches you visit if you're hoping to work on your tan."

"That's fine because I don't tan. I just burn."

"I bet you look like the lobsters we just ate!" Sophie said excitedly as she bumped him with her shoulder.

"Those were crabs."

She burst into a laugh and shook her head at her mistake. "I take it you didn't plan to come here for the sunshine, anyway."

"You're right. I didn't." Cole rested the flowers on the towel and pulled his glasses from his face to wipe the ocean fog from the lenses. He settled them back onto the bridge of his nose and leaned toward Sophie. Her inquisitive, green eyes searched his, darting rapidly back and forth. "I've learned a lot from you this last month, Sophie. Especially when it comes to the meaning of things." Cole reached out to lightly graze her cheek with his finger. He traced the line of her jaw to her chin as he gazed at her openly in awe. "Like flowers. These zinnias? I didn't choose them just because they're pretty. I chose them for what they represent. What they mean. Do you know what that is?"

Sophie glanced away and squinted out at the great stretch of water. She tapped her chin as she pondered for a brief moment, then said, "Remembrance, I think. *Daily* remembrance. Thinking of someone who's not here."

Cole nodded. "Fifteen years ago today, I lost my brother to this ocean, and there hasn't been a day since that I haven't thought about him."

"Oh, Cole. I had no idea—" Sophie's body stiffened at Cole's side.

"We were on a family vacation in Maui. I was a sophomore in high school and Caleb had just graduated. We'd taken off for a night swim. Mom and Dad were both sore from their sunburns and my sister, Trista, had just met a boy, so she was out with his family," Cole said. "I thought Caleb was playing around at first. We swam out pretty far from the beach and he mentioned he was getting tired. I gave him a hard time about his inability to tread water. I teased that it was the reason he got cut from the water polo team. It all happened so fast, Sophie. It was so dark. I looked for him for what felt like forever, struggling against the waves that took him under."

Moving closer, Sophie pressed her head to Cole's shoulder and wove her hand into his. That small gesture made Cole lose his breath.

"I carried around a lot of guilt for a long time. I think that's why I've worked so hard to fill Caleb's shoes with the business and with my dad. Up until recently, I felt like it was my fault. Like I should have been able to save him. I know that's not the case now, but it doesn't keep me from wondering what life would've been like if he was still here."

"Cole, I'm so sorry. I can't even imagine what you went through. I wish I had words to say that could make this all better for you."

"I'm not looking for that anymore. This trip out here has made me realize that Caleb wouldn't want me to live out his future. He would want me to make my own. I'm certain of that now." Cole swallowed, his voice straining. "I want a life out here, Sophie. I want to explore California and us and an existence that feels so much more like home than the one I had back in Nashville."

"Cole."

He swung his legs underneath his body and swiveled to face Sophie. Cupping her face in his large, strong hands, he said, "I'm falling in love with you, Sophie. And I want a future with you. Part of that is letting you into my past."

"I want a future with you, too." Pressing forward, her lips met his in a gentle kiss. "Thank you for trusting me with your past, Cole. I'm so sorry you've lived with this heartache for so long."

"Truthfully, my heart has never felt more healed." He leaned forward to draw her fully into his arms. "I have you to thank for that. I do wish things didn't have to start off so rocky for us, though, you know? I know the reason we met was the contest, but it sure has made things complicated."

"About that..." Sophie pulled back, her eyes locking with Cole's.

"Do you have news to tell me?"

"Not yet, just know that something is in the works that might make everyone happy in the end."

"Is this something I can help you with at all?"

Sophie grinned and pressed a palm to Cole's chest. "I know how much you love helping me, Cole, I do. But this is something I need to do on my own."

"Alright. I get that," he relented with an understanding nod. He grabbed ahold of the flowers and then Sophie's hand. "But I have something I need to do, and in this case, I would like your help."

19

SOPHIE

THERE WERE FIFTEEN flowers, one for every year Caleb had been gone. Sophie watched as Cole closed his eyes before casting each zinnia into the waves. Some would float for a minute before succumbing to the salty ocean depths. It took a half hour to toss out each one and Sophie felt drawn closer to Cole with every passing minute.

She admired his vulnerability and considered it a gift to be part of this ceremony. They had undoubtedly shared a lot during their new relationship, but this was a different level of openness. Cole had let her completely in. She wouldn't take that for granted. She made a promise to herself to reciprocate that vulnerability in any way she could.

After the final flower was cast into its watery resting place, Cole shoved his hands into his pockets and rocked back into the sand on his heels. Face skyward, his eyes fell shut as he pulled in a full, renewing breath of ocean air.

When he opened his eyes again, they were rimmed with red and wet with unspent tears.

"Thank you, Sophie." He glanced over and offered a thoughtful smile.

"You're welcome. Though I didn't really do much."

"But you did, just in being here," Cole said. "I needed your support today and you gave it to me, no questions asked. I don't know that I've ever had someone do that for me."

"I trust you, Cole. That's why I hopped in the car without knowing where we were going or what we were planning to do. My heart trusts yours."

"To hear you say that means everything to me. I knew the moment I met you that you were passionate. I remember thinking if you could live life so fully, you must love deeply, too. And that's what I felt from you today, Sophie. I felt loved," Cole confessed. They paced down the beach, watching the ocean waves continue their relentless back and forth dance with the shore, the consistency a comfort. "I'm not even necessarily talking about love in the romantic sense. If all I ever got from you was friendship, that friendship would be enough for me."

Sophie laughed a little under her breath. "Of course I'm happy to be your friend, Cole, but I can't honestly say I'd be okay with only that."

"Then I hope it's not too forward of me to say I want to pursue this." He fluttered his free hand back and forth in the space between them. "I want to see where things can go between us, Sophie. And I don't want to do that while living on opposite parts of the country."

Sophie froze. Her feet planted in the sand. "What are you getting at, Cole?"

He turned to take hold of her other hand, facing her. "I want to move to California. To Fairvale. I always thought this trip was meant to show my dad that I'm capable of taking over his business, but it's actually shown me I'm capable of starting my own. I want to make a life for myself out here, Sophie, and I want you to be a part of it."

Rising up on her toes, Sophie wrapped her arms around Cole's neck and let her agreement be known in a slow, tender kiss. She had fallen for this man, hesitantly at first, but now, after this declaration, she could let her guard fully down. She didn't have to protect her heart anymore. He wouldn't be taking it across the country with him after all.

They spent another hour at the beach, huddled together under the towel for warmth and shelter from the coastal breeze. Seagulls soared above, dipping down into the foamy ocean and shooting skyward like wild kites on a windy day. An older couple walked by and smiled. Sophie longed to know their story. She wanted to know all of the pages written in the life that led them to this spot on this beach in this particular point in time. It looked like they had created a beautiful one.

The ride back to Fairvale was quiet, peaceful. Cole gripped tightly to Sophie's hand on the armrest between them and every so often, he would look over and smile, his eyes alight with new affection. She knew Cole was taking a big risk with this proposed move out west. Taking a risk on her. But sitting there, side by side, traveling these California roads together, Sophie knew the biggest risk of all would be in not pursuing a future together.

That was a risk she just wasn't willing to take.

~

HE PICKED UP on the first ring. Sophie figured it would go straight to voicemail, so she startled at the sound of his low voice reverberating on the line. She hadn't quite prepared what she wanted to say. It was late and her thoughts were sleepy and jumbled.

"Sophie, what are you doing calling at this hour?"

"Please don't tell me you were already in bed. I'm going to feel really bad if you were."

"You're right. I wasn't." Scott chuckled. He was always one to give her a hard time. "What's up, sis?"

"Do you have a minute? There's something I need to talk to you about—something I've wanted to talk about for a long time, actually."

"Oh boy. Why do I feel a lecture coming on?"

"Not a lecture. More like a cautionary tale."

"Should I get a bag of popcorn started? Heat up a cup of coffee? I have a sneaking suspicion this is going to take awhile."

Sophie ignored the sarcasm. "I shared an emotional afternoon with someone today, Scott. Someone who's become pretty important in my life."

"Is this special someone named Cole?"

"How did you—?"

"Mom's told me all about him. Well, mostly about his glasses, but I've heard a bit about the guy."

"Yes. Cole," Sophie said. "Today was the fifteen-year anniversary of his brother's passing."

"Shoot, Sophie, I'm sorry to hear that."

"He hasn't been able to speak to his brother for fifteen years, Scott. *Fifteen.* And how many years have you and Derek let go by?"

"Listen, that's not all me—"

Sophie cut him off before he could make the flimsy excuse. "I know that. And I'm not calling you to point fingers or place blame. Today I glimpsed what it's like when you can't reach out to someone you love, and Scott, let me tell you, it's devastating. I'm not naïve enough to think Cole and his brother never had any problems or arguments. I'm sure they did. Family can be messy. But I know he would give anything to have just one more day with Caleb. And here you and Derek are, letting all of these days pass between you."

There was a pause. Sophie knew this sort of conversation was best done in person, but the immediacy of her plea didn't allow for that. She had to get it all out now. She had learned an invaluable lesson from Cole today, and it was one she had to share.

"You need to be here for the wedding, Scott," she continued. "I know Derek wasn't there for yours, and I don't condone any part of his behavior in that, but it's the right thing to do. One of you has to give and I think you've been presented an opportunity here to be the bigger man."

"There's no question I'm the bigger man," Scott said in jest. He was silent a moment before he added, "But I do agree with you, sis."

"Wait...What? You do?"

"Yeah. It's why I boarded the first flight from Seattle to Sacramento this morning."

Sophie's jaw dropped. "You what?"

"I'm over at Mom and Dad's now. Starving, by the way. That woman's cooking seems to get worse with age."

Sophie couldn't believe it. "You're seriously in Fairvale?"

"I seriously am. Shayna stayed back with Aimee since

she's still got a runny nose and the flight would be too painful with all that head congestion, but I'm here. For what it's worth, I suppose."

"It's worth more than you even know, Scott."

"I'm glad you think so, but I can't help but wonder if Derek will feel the same," Scott said. "I keep replaying this mental image of me getting kicked out of the wedding ceremony. Drug out by my hands and feet and thrown to the curb."

"Weddings aren't night clubs, Scott. There isn't going to be a bouncer checking I.D. at the church entrance."

He laughed heartily. "I suppose you're right."

"Does Derek know you're here?"

"No. Just Mom and Dad. And now you."

"Are you going to tell him ahead of time, or just show up at the church?"

Scott sighed. "That's where I will defer to your better judgment."

"Considering there is a whole *RSVP*-ing process for a wedding, my best advice would be to let Derek know before Saturday. At the very least, so he has a heads up for his caterer since there will be an additional mouth to feed."

"I hadn't really thought about that." Sophie could detect the vacillation in her brother's voice. "My just showing up does throw a monkey wrench in things, doesn't it? I don't want to cause more stress for him on his wedding day, sis. I really don't. Maybe I should've just stayed in Seattle and left things as they were. Seems like the easier option."

"Of course it's the easier option. Difficult things are difficult, Scott, but it doesn't mean they shouldn't be done."

"Difficult things are difficult. Where did you ever pick up such a profound piece of wisdom?"

"I'm being serious. I've had to make a few of my own difficult decisions lately, so I know what I'm talking about here," Sophie asserted.

"And what decisions are those? Which color of flower to plant? What type of fertilizer to use?"

"I'm selling my truck."

Sophie could almost hear Scott's jaw drop. "The one you spent three years restoring with the money you got from Grandma Sarah's inheritance? Soph, why would you do that?"

"An opportunity came up and I need the cash."

"But it's your truck. You love that thing."

"I know. It's not the ideal situation, believe me, but unless you happen to know where I can get thirty thousand dollars by Monday, I'm afraid it's my only option. Plus, I've already found a buyer, so at least that part of the process is done."

Scott sighed. "Man, when did being adults become so hard?"

"I wouldn't say you and Derek have been behaving anything like adults. The opposite actually. Sometimes it feels like you two have yet to grow up."

"Well, maybe me being here is the first step in that direction. How does the saying go? The journey of a thousand miles begins with a single step? So maybe the journey toward adulthood begins with a baby step."

"Sure. Something like that," Sophie said, choking back a laugh.

"Hey, it's catchier than difficult things are difficult."

"If you're done giving me a hard time, I'm going to

head to bed. It's been a long day and tomorrow's going to be even longer. I've got to get all of the flowers harvested so I can start on the arrangements for Saturday. I should try to get some rest."

"I should go, too. Mom and Dad just started a movie and if I don't at least pretend to be asleep, I'll get stuck listening to them bicker over the name of the actor that neither of them knows, but both are certain they are right about," Scott said. "Thanks for calling, sis. I mean, even though I had already made the decision to do the right thing, it's good to know you care enough to try to put me in my place."

"You can always count on that, Scott. Always."

"And that's why I love you, sis."

∼

BRIAN TEXTED AT daybreak, saying he had just laced up his running shoes and was about to head over with a cashier's check in hand. While Sophie spent the previous night tossing and turning over the decision, her bed sheets as tangled as the warring emotions within her, she knew it was the right choice. It was the only one.

She awoke early for one last morning drive through town, ending up at her favorite coffee shop before any other Fairvale inhabitants had even opened their eyes to start the day. As she waited at the barista bar of Heirloom Coffee, a starburst of light glinting off her windshield caught her eye as it reflected through the storefront windows. It cast rainbow prisms all across the walls, the tables, the chairs. Sophie's chest filled with hope at the kaleidoscope of color and she took that as a sign. A promise. Oh, how she needed one that particular morning.

"We've had a lot of good memories together," she spoke aloud as she began the drive home. Reaching for her latte, she pulled in a slow, warming sip. "I know it feels like I'm trading you in for the land, but I promise that's not the case. When I first found you, you were dirty. Neglected. In need of tending to and loving on. But over time, you've been restored into something beautiful." As she quietly spoke within the confines of the cab, her vision blurred with the tears she struggled to hold back. "The flower farm—that restorative process is ongoing. Every season, the soil needs to be worked. The seeds need to be planted. Pruned and weeded. And then, finally, the flowers will grow, restoring the land to beauty once again. You're not unlike those flowers, but it's time for someone else to enjoy you."

As she pulled into her driveway, she could see Brian bounding up the sidewalk. With her palm, she wiped her cheeks and sniffed. Brian wore a broad smile as he threw his hand into the air for a wave. Sophie knew he was the right owner for her truck. There was no doubt. She saw the way his eyes lit up when he spoke of the heartfelt memories made with his grandfather. The tone in his voice would change, nostalgia drawing out something real and true within him. He would take such good care of that truck and that was all Sophie could hope for.

"I'm still pinching myself over this," Brian admitted as Sophie climbed down from the vehicle to join him in the driveway. "My wife says I'm acting like a kid on Christmas morning, but I just can't help it."

"I'm so glad to hear that, Brian. I'm not going to lie; it

started out as a rough morning for me, but hearing your excitement makes it a little easier to let her go."

"I'm sure this wasn't an easy decision. I can tell you've put a lot of time into getting this truck where it is right now. I can assure you I'll continue to take good care of it. Might be the runner in me, but I look at this as a passing the baton sort of thing."

Sophie smiled. "I like that." She settled the keys into Brian's palm as he handed her the check in exchange. "I hope you take her to the finish line."

"Oh believe me—I have no intention of ever parting with this beauty. My dad says his biggest regret was selling Grandpa's truck after he passed. My hope is that I'll be able to make memories with my future grandkids. This truck is going to have a legacy. A true, lasting legacy."

Sophie didn't doubt it. In fact, she believed it already had one.

20

COLE

"THANK GOODNESS YOU'RE here!"

Caroline reached out and grabbed Cole's shirtsleeve, yanking him off of the front stoop and into the townhome. He had to concentrate not to spill the contents of the two coffee cups in his hands, her grip forceful and sudden.

Immediately, Cole could see the kitchen was a disaster. Bowls, pans, measuring cups, and mixers were strewn about like an earthquake shook them from their cupboards. And there was Caroline, covered in powdery white, caught in a confectionary snowstorm.

"Flour mishap?"

"Wedding cake mishap is more like it." She lifted the hem of her apron to her face and swiped her cheeks. "The wedding is tomorrow, Cole. *Tomorrow!* That's one day away. And do you know how many cakes I've gone through so far?"

"I'm guessing more than one?"

"Three." Behind her, several crumbled cakes littered the counter. "Three cakes! And none of them are right. I knew I was taking on more than I could handle with this, but I just had to do it, you know? I couldn't let someone else bake my wedding cake when it's what I do. I'm a baker. It would be like having someone else landscape your yard."

"I get it, Caroline," Cole said. "But I also know we tend to be much harder on ourselves than others are. My guess is these failed cakes aren't as bad as you think."

"Oh, they're bad. Very bad."

"Mind if I try a bite?"

Caroline closed her eyes and shook her head as though downright defeated. "Only if you don't place any real value on your taste buds." Grabbing one of the coffee cups from Cole's hand, she guzzled down the hot latte meant for Sophie. Cole didn't protest. He figured the bride-to-be needed it more than her roommate. "I'm not kidding, Cole. I've never made anything so terrible in my life. It's like I've completely forgotten everything I've ever known about baking."

Stepping around her, Cole withdrew a fork from the cutlery drawer and dug into the first deconstructed cake. It was a rich brown, chocolaty in appearance.

Squinting one eye shut, Caroline awaited the verdict.

"It's…" Cole tried to keep his face neutral as he chewed on the spongy texture. "It's not completely terrible."

"That's exactly what I mean!" Caroline grabbed the fork, shoved a heaping bite into her mouth, and then promptly spit it into the sink. "*How was Caroline and Derek's wedding?*" she said in a fabricated, nasally voice.

"*The ceremony was lovely and the cake wasn't completely terrible!*"

"No one is going to say that," Cole assured.

"You're right. They won't. Because they won't be able to talk since all of their taste buds will have been totally destroyed!"

"I'm not sure that's how it works—"

"Cole! What am I going to do?" Collapsing onto the counter, Caroline buried her face in her folded arms and let out a gargled yelp.

Cole moved to the second cake in the line of discarded pans. This wasn't as bad as the first, but something was still off. His mouth watered, the bite of acid tickling his tongue. "Are you following a recipe for these?"

"I don't really use recipes. It's all up here." She lifted her head and tapped it with her index finger. "Hasn't failed me yet. Until today, of course."

Unwilling to spit out the inedible cake in front of Caroline, Cole choked down the contents in his mouth. That was rough. There was no doubt something was amiss with the ingredients. Glancing around the kitchen, Cole took inventory. Cocoa powder, flour, baking soda, cinnamon. Stepping closer, he squinted at two rectangular containers placed side by side, their lids off and left next to them on the tile. Cole picked up the covers and read their labels aloud.

"Salt and sugar, huh?"

"Yeah. Those go to the containers right there."

Lifting the lids, Cole swapped them back and forth between his hands, shuffling them like playing cards. "Does this one go to this? Or to this?"

Caroline's eyes bulged. "Oh no. You don't think I...?"

"I think maybe you did."

She flung her hands into the air. "Are you kidding me? Knowing the difference between salt and sugar is like knowing day from night. How on earth could I make that mistake not once, but *three* times?"

"I think maybe the fact that tomorrow is the big day might have a little something to do with it."

"I suppose," she relented as she slumped against the counter. "Some brides get cold feet; apparently I get wedding brain." Letting out a sigh, Caroline said, "Looks like I'll need to go to the store to get more ingredients since I've already wasted all of this." She waved her hand over the spread before them. "Any chance I can bum a ride off of you? Sophie's got my car over at the farm for the day."

"What happened to her truck?" Cole asked.

"Other than it not belonging to her anymore?"

"What?"

"She hasn't told you?"

"Told me what, Caroline?"

Gathering her purse from the counter, Caroline slung it over her shoulder, readying to go. "That she sold her truck."

"Sold her truck? Why would she do that?"

Caroline's lips straightened into a line. "Sounds like maybe this is a conversation you should have with Sophie and not me. But after you take me to the store. I have a wedding cake to bake!"

~

COLE TRIED SOPHIE'S cell phone three times with no

answer. The news that Caroline let slip still didn't seem plausible. There was no way Sophie would sell her truck. Cole knew how much she loved it, how much pride she took in its restoration. He wished she would have included him in that decision, but he knew it wasn't his to make.

If she had wanted his opinion, she would've asked for it. She hadn't, and Cole didn't know if he was justified in feeling the sting of that rejection.

"Come on, pick up," he said as it went to voicemail for the fourth time.

It wasn't a message Cole wanted to leave in a recording. Instead, he drove out to the farm, determined to hear the truth of the situation from Sophie herself.

Tanner's SUV was parked just behind Caroline's car, and another vehicle Cole didn't recognize was across the street. Sitting there in his driver's seat, Cole tried to collect his thoughts and put them in an order that made sense.

When they were at the beach, Sophie mentioned a solution that would make everyone happy. He just couldn't see how parting with her beloved truck would result in her happiness. That's all that he wanted for Sophie. For her to be truly happy. This decision seemed like a rash one and he wished he'd been given the chance to give it some weight.

"Hey there, boss!" Tanner bounded up and hooked his hands on the door, poking his head through Cole's rolled down passenger window. "Didn't know if I'd see you out here today."

"Is Sophie here?"

"Yep. Working on centerpieces for the wedding, I think."

"Good. I need to talk to her," Cole said.

"Oh, I figured you were here to talk to your dad."

"My dad?"

Tanner slapped his hand on the door, almost like a high five. "Yep. Great guy. I see now that the apple doesn't fall far from the tree. Anyway, I'm gonna go grab some lunch. Can I get you anything?"

Stunned, Cole had a difficult time forming the words, "No, thank you. I'm good."

"Alrighty. I'll see you when I get back if you're still here."

Cole sat speechless for several minutes. His father was in Fairvale? Why hadn't he told him about his plans to visit? A sick, familiar feeling tugged at him, like when his dad would hover over Cole as he did homework, just waiting to point out an error or correction needing to be made. Though he was a grown man, Cole still sought his father's approval, likely always would.

Clearing his throat, he stepped out of the car and made his way over to the yard. He could hear his dad's robust voice before he came into view. He always had a commanding presence, one that could be felt both near and far, even with the span of the entire Midwest between them.

"Tell Ralph I say hello next time you talk to him. I was hoping to catch up with him this trip, but it doesn't look like I'll have the time."

Cole could see the McAllisters, along with his father, Martin, standing in the very center of the property. The couple nodded. Kelly placed a hand on Martin's forearm while Theodore reached out for a cordial handshake. After they retreated to the house, Cole stood by, eyeing his father from several yards away.

He followed his dad's gaze as he took in the last month of Cole's life with one sweeping glance. A slow, yet perceptible nod was the only indicator that suggested any hint of approval.

"Dad," Cole called out as he edged closer. "Dad, what are you doing here?"

"Cole, there you are." His father looked surprised to see him, something Cole couldn't place considering this piece of land was his workplace. "Wasn't sure if I'd run into you here."

"Here, as in California? Or here, at the jobsite?"

"Cole, this turned out so nicely. An impressive project to add to your portfolio."

"Is that why you're here, Dad? To sign off on things? To check in on me?"

His father brought his hand up to smooth his beard, a habit Cole once thought was unintentional, but now realized stood as a smokescreen. There was more to his dad's sudden arrival, and Cole wanted answers.

"The McAllisters are so happy with it, too. You have a real knack for this, son."

"Thank you, but so far everything you've said could've been relayed in a text or a phone call. Why are you here, Dad?"

Looking over at the porch chairs under the pergola, Martin Blankenship nodded. "Sit with me a moment, son."

Cole could feel his pulse beat frantically in his neck, his palms coated with sweat.

Martin sat first, then Cole. "Yesterday was a hard day for me."

Cole hoped his father wouldn't forget the calendar

date, and hearing that he did remember made him feel a little less alone in his grief.

"I can't believe Caleb has been gone for fifteen years," his father continued. "You know, yesterday made me do a lot of reflecting. About the firm. About you."

"It wasn't an easy day for me either, Dad."

"I know that, Cole, I do. And I know there have been many other days in between that haven't been easy. I realize I'm to blame for some of those." His dad squinted out into the distance, his prominent, gray brow pulling tightly over deep-set, charcoal eyes. "I pushed you into the role your brother was supposed to take on with the business. I know you're aware of that. And you haven't given me any grief for it. You just did your job. And you've done it well. This project is a testament to that."

Cole didn't know what to say. He just sat there, taking in his father's words, letting them settle into his head and his heart.

"I've had every intention of handing the business over to you, Cole, I have. But something about yesterday made me change my mind. I don't want you to take on something that was never meant to be yours. The firm was my dream, and then it was Caleb's. I'll be retiring next year, and when I do, it'll be the end of Blankenship Backyard Designs."

"You don't need to close down the business, Dad."

"But I do. I need to release you from the expectation that it's your responsibility to take over the firm. The only way I know to do that is to take away the firm altogether."

"But I like working for you. This project has been incredible—"

"And you've done it *all on your own*, Cole. This is the

first project where I haven't been there, breathing down your neck every step of the way. And look at it. It's magnificent."

The compliment cut straight into Cole in the very best way. "I don't know what to say, Dad."

"I don't really either, Cole. But I do know if this is something you want to pursue with your life, you should do it. I'll be there to support you in any way possible. I just want to make sure I'm supporting *your* dream, not one someone else has passed down to you."

Cole breathed deep, filling his lungs to capacity. This information was a lot to take in. "I think I want to do this here, actually. I've grown to love California and I've met some pretty remarkable people along the way. I'm not ready to part with that."

"Would one of those people be that beautiful young flower farmer across the way?"

Martin glanced toward the field at Sophie who stood among the blossoming rows with her clippers in hand and a floppy sunhat perched on her head.

"Yes," Cole answered, his heart swelling at the sight of her. "But I don't know the first thing about starting my own company, Dad. And even if I wanted to, I don't have the capital to do it."

"I just so happen to know someone who will be retiring soon who might have a little extra investment money coming his way." Martin's large hand dropped onto his son's knee. "I'm happy to invest in your dreams, Cole. And I'm supportive of you living them out here, if that's what you want. I just don't want to be your boss anymore. We've had too many years of that and I want a new start between us. A new relationship. Just father and son."

"I want that, too, Dad. I've always wanted that."

Martin turned. "I love you, Cole. I don't say it often enough—if ever, really—but I do."

"I love you, too, Dad."

Between the love he'd always had for the man sitting beside him and the growing love he had for the woman across the field, Cole wasn't sure his heart had ever felt so full.

Fairvale had opened up Cole in ways he'd never imagined, and regardless of the backyard contest outcome, Cole knew he had already won in all of the ways that truly mattered.

21

SOPHIE

"AND WHAT ARE these called?" Cole's father wrapped his fingers around the stem of a coral colored bloom and brought his face closer as he sniffed the pollen-filled center.

"Those are zinnias, my personal favorite. Although they don't have much of a scent, do they?"

"I suppose a flower that looks like this doesn't really need to smell good, too," Martin said, chuckling. "Wouldn't be fair to all the other flowers to hog the most desirable qualities."

Sophie could see Cole's steady gaze out of her periphery. She knew exactly what he wanted to ask her. She could feel it in his questioning stare. Knowing that, she was more than a little grateful for Martin who served as a buffer and distraction.

Cole wouldn't understand, and worse, if he did understand, he would want to help. To talk her out of it. What was done was done and Sophie didn't regret it. Selling the truck was something she needed to do on her own.

"How many varieties do you have growing here, Sophie?"

"Oh, gosh. You know, I have a journal that lists everything I've planted, but I can't say I know the exact number. Probably upwards of thirty."

"And you're a florist, too?"

"Yep, a farmer florist. In fact, I'm just finishing up the centerpieces and bouquets for my brother's wedding tomorrow. I should probably get them home soon and into the cooler, actually. It's not terribly warm today, but I don't want them to wilt."

"We won't take up any more of your time then, will we Cole?"

Cole studied Sophie through his glasses and responded in a flat, "No, we won't."

Martin took Sophie's hands into his. "I sure hope I get to spend some more time with you before I head out on Sunday morning. I know Cole thinks quite highly of you and I can certainly see why."

"Why don't you join us for the rehearsal dinner tonight?" Sophie asked. "It would be a great time for you to meet some of Cole's new friends and I know there will be plenty of food to go around."

"I couldn't impose."

"It's not an imposition at all. It's at my favorite little Italian restaurant, Aromatizzare. You'll love it. Best manicotti in town."

"Well, that sounds very nice, Sophie. Thank you for the invitation. Count me in."

"Five o'clock," Sophie said. "Cole knows the place."

Cole's mouth lifted into a smile, but it fell away

quickly when his eyes locked with Sophie's. "Hey, Dad? You mind if I stay and chat with Sophie for a bit?"

Martin nodded. "Not a problem at all. I'm going to head to the hotel, anyway. Maybe take a nap. I'm still exhausted from that redeye. I just can't fall asleep on planes, even if it's the middle of the night," he said. "It was great meeting you, Sophie. I look forward to this evening."

"I do, too, Mr. Blankenship."

"It's just Martin," he said, smiling as he turned to go. "I'll catch up with you later, Cole."

"Sounds good, Dad."

The two waited until Cole's father had retreated back toward the street. The flowers surrounding them rustled together, their leaves brushing as the breeze made them bend and sway. Cole didn't take his eyes off of Sophie and she could feel the weight of his gaze like a physical force.

"Why did you sell your truck?"

"I knew this was coming."

"Sophie, why didn't you tell me?"

"Because I didn't want to be talked out of it." She lifted her shoulders to her ears in a shrug and then dropped them back down and huffed out a breath. "Two weeks from now, I'll own the deed to this land." She stomped a foot on the ground. "This land, Cole. It'll be mine, free and clear. But in order to make that happen, I needed the cash and my truck was the only way to get it."

"The McAllisters are selling? How did you work that out?"

"Let's just say it took some sweet talking, along with some actual sweets. Turns out they had plans to parcel off the land years ago and went through all of the steps with the county, but then bowed out at the last minute. It only required a few final signatures and a few more pulled strings, but it should be signed off on by Monday. Then, after a ten-day escrow, I will have officially bought the farm."

"Sophie—"

"I know, Cole, I know. I should have told you but I—"

"I was actually going to say how proud I am of you." He placed his hands on her arms and pulled her closer.

"Proud of me?"

"Yeah. I love your independence and your drive. You see something you want and you just go for it. It's inspiring."

"You love it?"

He lowered his face so his lips were just inches from hers. She could feel his warm breath on her skin. "I do. Along with everything else about you."

With the softest touch, Cole's mouth met Sophie's in a slow, sweet kiss. A tingling shiver ran up and down her spine, her head light and dizzied. It wasn't quite an *I love you*, but she could feel his affection in every ounce of her being.

～

"HOW WONDERFUL IS it to have all of my family under one roof?" Geri held up her crystal glass in a toast. Aromatizzare buzzed with conversation and pre-wedding jitters, a palpable energy that filled the room like helium. "Well, all but Shayna and that sweet grandbaby of mine." She thrust her glass higher into the air. "To family!"

"To family!" Everyone cheered. Glasses met together in a cacophony of clinking.

With the weight of Cole's arm resting protectively across the back of her chair, Sophie sat deeply in her seat, taking in the face of every guest that surrounded the banquet table. To see her brothers not only in the same room, but seated side by side, was shocking. There was still a perceptible strain between them, but they had exchanged amicable words rather than fists, and that, in and of itself, was nothing short of a miracle. Sophie knew it would take time to rebuild the bridge they had so badly burned, but she was hopeful for that restorative process. As Scott had said, one baby step at a time.

Caroline lifted her glass next. "Here's to salty cakes that keep you humble!"

"Cheers!" they all agreed, though the meaning of her toast was lost on Sophie.

"And here's to finding the love of your life, proposing, and having her agree to spend the rest of your lives growing wrinkly and old together," Derek said as he leaned in to kiss his fiancé on the cheek.

Whether intentional or not, Sophie couldn't help but feel the small squeeze of Cole's hand upon her shoulder. Heart hammering, she kept her gaze trained forward, knowing if she glanced his way, her heated and red cheeks would tell him all too clearly that she felt it.

"To Derek and Caroline," Sophie's father said, rising to stand. "Thank you all so much for being here tonight." He turned toward Caroline's mother and father who sat at the opposite end of the long table. "George and Patty, you have raised a beautiful young woman in Caroline and our family is so blessed that we finally get to call her our daughter. There's nothing more meaningful than the joining of two families in love. Thank you for welcoming us into yours. We look forward to many more dinners of celebration just like this one."

Patty and George raised their glasses.

"Well, that's all for now everyone, but please feel free to stick around to enjoy some more pasta. There's plenty of it," Jerry continued. "Otherwise I'll be left eating it for the next week."

"Which wouldn't be such a bad thing, considering someone's cooking," Derek muttered, but audibly enough for everyone to hear.

"Oh, quiet you!" Geri snapped her son with a whip of her napkin. "Just because you're going to be a married man tomorrow doesn't mean you can start talking to your mother that way."

"You know I love you, Mom," Derek said. "Just not your cooking."

"I'd like to say something before we all head out." Speaking up for the first time that evening, Scott cleared his throat and scooted his chair out. Sophie could see his drink slosh in its cup, his unsteady hand trembling.

"Of course, son." Jerry tipped his head in a nod. "Go right ahead."

"I know it's been awhile since I've been back to Fair-vale, but there really is nothing like coming home. The memories I've made here—both good and bad—I've kept those with me as I started a new life in Seattle. But there's one memory in particular that stands out."

"The Great Forgiveness Pact," Derek and Sophie said in unison.

"I had a feeling you guys might remember." Scott

laughed. "For those who don't know what we're talking about, back when we were kids—gosh, this was over twenty years ago, at least—we broke Mom's antique cookie jar. Smashed it to smithereens. Man, she loved that jar. I think it belonged to her mother."

"My grandmother, actually," Geri corrected.

"Right. Your grandma. Well, the crazy thing is, I don't even remember which one of us broke it. All I can recall is creating this elaborate plan to ask for Mom's forgiveness." Across the table, Sophie's parents nodded their heads, the memory gradually coming back to them, as well. "I wrote the script, of course, and Derek memorized it to present it to Mom, in true anchorman fashion. And Sophie had the idea to give her a bouquet because in her words, flowers always made everything better."

"And I still stand by those words," Sophie chimed in. "But probably not the manner in which I got those particular flowers."

"Right," Scott said. "If memory serves me correctly, you lopped off Mrs. Frankfurt's daffodils, the ones her late husband had planted as bulbs the year before. Not sure Mrs. Frankfurt ever did accept our apology for that." Scott paused. "Anyway, what strikes me most about this memory isn't that I would one day turn into a writer, Derek would actually become an anchorman, and Sophie would —in fact—become a flower farmer. What always stands at the forefront of my mind is that we were a team and our goal was forgiveness. Somehow, over time and through actions I take a lot of responsibility for, that team pulled apart."

Sophie could feel her throat go raw. She grinned up at

her brother affectionately, encouraging him to continue. She had waited for this day for so long.

"Caroline, you've got a great teammate in Derek, you do. But speaking as a married man, forgiveness—and the humility to ask for it—is the foundation of any great relationship. If you can practice daily forgiveness, you can and will get through anything."

"Here, here!" Derek said as he stood to his feet and draped an arm around his brother. "To forgiveness!"

"To forgiveness."

"And to getting to bed at a decent hour the night before your wedding so you don't look like a zombie bride on the biggest day of your life!" Caroline exclaimed, looking at her wristwatch in panic.

"Oh goodness, it's ten o'clock already!" Geri said. "How did it get so late?"

Chairs scraped across the wood planked floor as family members stood from the dinner table. Guests gathered in clusters of conversation as others excused themselves for the night, thanking the Potters for hosting such a lovely evening. Cole took Sophie's hand into his and guided her off to the side of the noisy room where they could be alone.

"Thank you for inviting me here tonight," he said in a lowered voice.

"Of course. You're my plus one."

"I like that." He beamed. "You have an amazing family, Sophie. I already knew that, but tonight just solidified it for me."

"A family you should do everything in your power to become a part of, son." Martin came up behind Cole and squeezed his shoulders. He slapped a palm to his back, the way Sophie's dad often did with his sons.

Cole's face went red, just like a sunburn.

"I'm headed back to the hotel for now, but I'll catch up with you both after the wedding. I know you have a busy day ahead of you, Sophie," Martin said.

"Actually, all of the hard work is already done. Tomorrow I just get to enjoy the celebration."

"As it should be," Martin noted, enveloping Sophie in a fatherly hug. He leaned back and looked at her with kind, thoughtful eyes. "Take care of my boy, will you?"

"Absolutely," Sophie agreed. She smiled up at Cole who wore a look of complete adoration on his face. She was certain hers reflected just the same. "Always."

"And you take good care of Sophie, son. Do not let this one get away. I know I told you I would support you in any way possible with this move out to California, but if I hear of you doing anything to lose this incredible woman, all bets are off. Understood?"

"Understood, Dad." Looking down only at Sophie, Cole's reverent gaze all but took her breath away. He drew her into his chest in the fiercest of hugs as he said, "I don't plan to ever let her go."

ONE YEAR LATER

"WHAT IS CAROLINE's current favorite? Mint chocolate chip or mocha almond fudge?"

Cole held up two cartons of ice cream.

"Neither," Sophie said as she took both from his hands and placed them back into the freezer case. "Neapolitan." Scanning the frozen food section, her gaze landed on the flavor in question. She tossed the half gallon into their shopping cart. "I honestly think each week of her pregnancy could be marked by a different ice cream craving."

"At least. But don't forget that short window where she only ate potatoes. Scalloped. Twice Baked. Mashed."

"French fries," Sophie continued, giggling. She pulled her shopping list from her purse and scanned the items written on it. "Okay. Looks like the only thing left is the dressing for the salad. That's a couple aisles over, I think, with the croutons. We should probably pick up an extra box of those, too."

Taking hold of the cart, Sophie maneuvered through

the crowds. The grocery store was always busy on week-
ends, but with her flower harvesting schedule and Cole's
work week, it left Saturday morning as the only day for
errands. Tonight they had plans to host Caroline and Derek
for dinner at Sophie's townhome. Her sister-in-law was
due in just under a week, and Sophie knew once her little
nephew made his debut, their family dinners would be few
and far between.

She looked down at her list again and startled when the
cart came to an abrupt stop.

Letting out a yelp, the woman in front of her grabbed
her heel, wincing. When she turned around, Sophie's face
immediately flushed with embarrassment. "Tammy! I'm so
sorry! I wasn't looking where I was going!"

Her brother's co-host strained to smile through gritted
teeth as she continued rubbing her ankle. "Sophie," she
said, then looked to Cole standing off to the side. "Cole.
So nice to see you both."

"You too, Tammy," Sophie said. "Is your ankle okay? I
honestly just wasn't paying attention. I'm so sorry."

Tammy swatted at Sophie like she was an annoying fly.
"It's fine." Nothing in her clenched tone indicated it was
fine, but Sophie knew better than to keep apologizing.
Groveling was not necessary when something was a
complete accident. "Cole, I was so surprised I didn't see
your name on the entry list for the backyard competition
this year. I know you've been quite successful getting your
landscape design firm up and running here in Fairvale. I
thought you'd be on that list, for sure."

"Once was enough for me," Cole said. He hooked his
hands on Sophie's shoulders possessively and squeezed. "I
got all I needed from it."

"But you were so close last year with second place. Didn't want to try again for first?"

"Nope."

"Well, that's a shame. It would've been nice to have you in the competition again. Our loss. Maybe next year?"

"Maybe," was all Cole said as Tammy smiled and said her obligatory goodbyes. Sophie tried to ignore the slight limp in Tammy's step as she headed toward the checkout stand.

"I feel terrible that I clipped her with the cart."

"Oh, don't feel bad. Tammy's dramatic. Remember how she acted when she read last year's winner? You would've thought she was announcing the Best Picture at the Oscars."

"And the look on her face when it wasn't the McAllister property that won," Sophie recalled. She turned the cart down another aisle and browsed the shelves for her favorite Italian dressing.

"At some point we should stop calling it the McAllister property. Derek and Caroline have owned it for almost ten months."

"The Potters' property does have a better ring to it, doesn't it?"

Sophie stretched up to grab a bottle from the top shelf, but Cole stepped in to pull it down for her. He placed it in the basket of the cart.

"I can't believe I've owned my portion of it for a year now. I'm still pinching myself over how everything turned out in the end," Sophie continued.

Leaning down to steal a kiss, Cole said, "I pinch myself every single day."

"Surprised you haven't given yourself a bruise yet."

"Nope, just butterflies."

"You're silly." Sophie leaned into Cole's side. "Let's get finished up here so we can head back to my house. I can't wait to get my hands dirty with our newest project."

"In fairness, Soph, your hands are always dirty."

"Well, that just goes with the flower farming territory!"

∽

SOPHIE SCOOTED OUT from underneath the truck, the wheels of the creeper rolling like skates across the garage floor. The smell of oil and grime and rust filled the tight space and it took her instantly back to long days spent restoring her treasured truck in this very garage. She loved that a scent could transport her so easily in that way.

"Hand me the wire brush for the drill?" she asked as she peered up at Cole who hovered just over the open hood. He was so handsome with his squared jaw, glasses, and the permanent smile he always seemed to have for her. Even the fresh stripe of grease that crossed his cheek made him all the more endearing.

Cole walked to the nearby table, grabbed the brush, and then handed off the attachment. Sophie fit it to the power tool and pulled the trigger to make the brush spin.

"There's a lot of rust under here, Cole."

"I figured there would be. This might be a bigger restoration than your last one. I remembered it being in better shape when I asked Dad to have it shipped out west."

"I'm always up for a challenge," Sophie said, rolling back under the truck. The drill squealed again as she began scraping at the underbelly of the vehicle. It would take months to get this truck road worthy, but neither Cole, nor Sophie, cared about the timeframe. It was an undertaking born from love and shared interests and they both knew working on it together would only bring them closer.

Cole looked down at Sophie, at her legs and sneaker-clad feet that peeked out from the classic truck. He'd had a knot in his throat all morning and afternoon and nothing he did could loosen it.

"Can you grab that undercoat spray for me?" Sophie's voice hollered over the pulsing drill. "I want to test out a small portion here and see how it takes it."

Cole made deliberately loud steps toward the toolbox, but when he came back, he held something else entirely in his hands.

"Were you able to find it for me?" she asked after a long stretch of quiet. She waved a hand out from under the truck. "Cole?"

Rolling out, Sophie's eyes fell wide open at the sight of the man she loved, down on one knee, a single red rose in his hands.

"Sophie—"

"Cole? What are you...?" She sat up on the rolling board, now face to face.

"Sophie, when I came out to California, I wasn't hoping to find love," he began through a strained voice. "I was hoping to find success. And I did find that, along with a new definition for it. For me, success is no longer measured in money or jobs, but in the love you've created and the joy your life brings. And Sophie, my life has never been more joy-filled than when I'm with you, here in Fairvale."

"Cole." Sophie gasped as she saw the glimmering

diamond ring peeking out from between the crimson petals. "Oh, Cole," she whispered again.

"Sophie Potters, will you marry me? Will you let me spend every season of every year of the rest of our lives loving you and nurturing you and caring for you? Our love has grown so much over the last year and I can't wait to see it continue to bloom."

"Yes, Cole!" she shouted. The rolling board shot out from underneath her as she flung herself forward and into his arms. "Yes, I will marry you!"

"Really?"

"Yes, really! Was there ever any doubt?"

"Doubt? No. I just wasn't sure if the timing was right, what with Derek and Caroline's baby coming later this week. I didn't want to steal their thunder."

"Steal their thunder? I'm not worried about that. But I will be stealing that ice cream of hers to celebrate. I'm going to go grab it from the freezer right now."

Cole took the sparkling ring from the folded petals and slipped it onto Sophie's finger. It was a perfect fit. "We won't have to do that. I've already got reservations for the four of us at Aromatizzare."

"Derek and Caroline knew?"

"Everyone knew." Cole laughed. He ran his hands up and down Sophie's back, holding her close, never wanting to let go. "Even your mom. I'm impressed she kept that a secret."

"You and me both." Sophie rolled her wrist back and forth, admiring the shine as the ring cast slivers of light across the garage walls like a disco ball. "I'm actually glad we're going out to eat. I was having a hard time getting excited about cooking that chicken casserole. But the

Lover's Special—that's something I can get excited about!"

"Me, too," Cole said. "Think you'll share with me this time?"

"Cole, I just agreed to share my entire life with you." She pulled him into a long kiss, then said, "I'll gladly share my dinner. But I get first dibs on the manicotti. You always take the biggest ones for yourself."

"Deal." Cole smiled at his fiancé, feeling more at home than ever before, knowing this feeling would exist no matter where they were. There had been a time when he thought home was a place, but Sophie showed him it was a person. It wasn't your address that mattered, but the space where your heart took up residence, and Cole's heart belonged with Sophie, now and forever.

"Let's get cleaned up," Sophie said, still staring appreciatively at her ring finger. "I feel like I'm not quite fancy enough for this ring just yet."

"That ring doesn't even hold a candle to your beauty, Sophie."

"You're just saying that."

"Have you ever known me to say anything that wasn't true?"

"No," Sophie said. "You're the most honest man I know, Cole. Which is why I love you and I trust you more than anyone. I can't wait to become Mrs. Blankenship."

Cole beamed. "That's the next big question—the wedding date. I figure we'll want to coordinate around your flower and market seasons."

Grabbing his face with her hands, Sophie stared deeply into Cole's eyes, a love and a desire unlike anything he'd experienced present in her gaze. "Cole, the only season in my life that matters from here on out is the one I'm about to embark on with you. You're the most important person in my entire world."

"Even more important than your flowers?"

"Even more important than my flowers. I love you, Cole. With everything within me."

"I love you, too, Sophie," Cole said, knowing this was what it felt like to win in both love and life. He would forever have Sophie, his new family and friends, and the town of Fairvale to thank for that.

THE END

ABOUT THE AUTHOR

Growing up with only a lizard for a pet, Megan Squires now makes up for it by caring for the nearly forty animals on her twelve-acre flower farm in Northern California. A UC Davis graduate, Megan worked in the political non-profit realm prior to becoming a stay-at-home mom. She then spent nearly ten years as an award winning photographer, with her work published in magazines such as Professional Photographer and Click.

In 2012, her creativity took a turn when she wrote and published her first young adult novel. Megan is both traditionally and self-published and *In the Market for Love* is her ninth publication. She can't go a day without Jesus, her family and farm animals, and a large McDonald's Diet Coke.

~

To stay up to date on new releases, sales, and cover reveals, please sign up for Megan's newsletter:

http://subscribe.megansquiresauthor.com

To keep up with Megan online, please visit:

 facebook.com/MeganSquiresAuthor

twitter.com/MeganSquires

Made in the USA
Monee, IL
06 January 2023

24667775R00142